"Sometimes you just have to go with the moment..."

"Shared intense experiences can create a false sense of attraction that is often misconstrued as something deeper," Hope said, lifting her chin.

"Interesting," J.T. said. "Care to put your theory to the test?"

"W-what do you mean?" she stammered, her eyes widening as he walked slowly toward her. "And it's not a theory. It's a proven scientific fact."

"So prove it," he said in a low tone, stalking her like a jungle cat. He backed her against the wall, trapping her within the space of his arms. She looked adorably perplexed and uncertain as to how to handle their close proximity.

He knew he ought to knock it off, and, in truth, he'd started this just to mess with her. But now that he was in her space, he was just as affected.

"We agreed to keep things professional," she reminded him in a breathy voice.

"I don't remember making that deal," he said, leaning in...

Dear Reader,

I've always wanted to write a story with a plane crash in a jungle. I don't know why this appeals to me so much, but I adore stories featuring this plot element. So when I struck upon an idea that involved this very thing, I was beyond excited.

What I didn't take into consideration was the immense amount of research I would have to do, seeing as I know next to nothing about the Amazon jungle aside from it is very dense and there are a million ways to die a grisly death.

All I can say is thank goodness for Google Earth.

However, it was a fun challenge to craft a fun, sexy and *wild* ride through the Amazon with two complete polar opposites for love interests.

I hope you laugh, bite your nails and blush when you read this story!

Enjoy.

Kim

Hearing from readers is a special joy. You can find me in the following places:

Website: kimberlyvanmeter.com

Facebook: Facebook.com/kim.vanmeter.37

Email: alexandria2772@hotmail.com

Snail mail: PO BOX 2210, Oakdale, CA 95361

Kimberly Van Meter

———

The Flyboy's Temptation

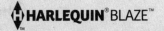

Recycling programs
for this product may
not exist in your area.

ISBN-13: 978-0-373-79898-8

The Flyboy's Temptation

Copyright © 2016 by Kimberly Sheetz

Printed in U.S.A.

www.Harlequin.com

Kimberly Van Meter wrote her first book at sixteen and finally achieved publication in December 2006. She writes for the Harlequin Superromance, Blaze and Romantic Suspense lines. She and her husband of seventeen years have three children, three cats and always a houseful of friends, family and fun.

Books by Kimberly Van Meter

Harlequin Blaze

The Hottest Ticket in Town
Sex, Lies and Designer Shoes
A Wrong Bed Christmas
"Ignited"

Harlequin Romantic Suspense

The Sniper
The Agent's Surrender
Moving Target

Harlequin Superromance

Family in Paradise

Like One of the Family
Playing the Part
Something to Believe In

The Sinclairs of Alaska

That Reckless Night
A Real Live Hero
A Sinclair Homecoming

To get the inside scoop on Harlequin Blaze and its talented writers, be sure to check out BlazeAuthors.com.

All backlist available in ebook format.

Visit the Author Profile page at Harlequin.com for more titles.

1

"Hello? Um, hello? Is there anyone here?"

James "J. T." Carmichael banged his head against the frame of his Beechcraft turboprop charter plane and swore a blue streak as he rubbed his dome.

"Who's asking?" he said, squinting against the blazing Southern California sun as his hangover made the pain of bumping his head that much worse. "If you're a creditor, then I ain't here."

A leggy redhead wearing a pencil skirt and spindly heels peered at him through dark-rimmed glasses. "Not a creditor…Mr.…"

J.T. straightened and wiped his hands on a dirty rag from his pocket, giving her the once-over just as openly.

He supposed she wasn't lying. He didn't know many creditors who actually showed up on a person's doorstep to collect. And heaven help him, creditors didn't look like her. Or at least, he hoped they didn't.

He'd rather think that creditors hung out in darkened cubicles, didn't shower and had complexions that reflected their junk-food diet. "J. T. Carmichael, co-owner of Blue Yonder. My brother, Teagan, is the other half. Is there something I can do for you?"

She pushed strands of fine red hair away from her china-doll face and straightened her glasses. "Mr. Carmichael, I'm in need of a charter to South America. Are you available?"

South America? That was a heckuva journey. Pricey, too.

Teagan's voice rang in his head from last night's argument alongside the pounding of his brain.

Teagan was in favor of calling it quits; J.T. wasn't ready to give up on their dream.

The numbers don't lie, J.T. We're going to be bankrupt in two months at this rate.

Why had he thought mixing Jack and tequila was a good idea?

Because the bartender had been hot.

"Mr. Carmichael?" The redhead's firm voice held an edge of impatience. "Are you capable of such a charter?"

Capable? Hell yes. But should he accept the job? His Spidey sense was tingling off the charts. Something wasn't right. And it wasn't just that this hot-looking chick was coming to his small operation when she plainly could afford something nicer. Although, now that he thought about it, that seemed a little off, too.

But hadn't Teagan groused that they'd need a miracle to keep the doors open? Hell, looked like a miracle wore fancy designer glasses and an air of mystery.

And who was he to look a gift horse in the mouth?

"Of course," he answered, eyeing her warily. "But that's a pretty expensive ride. Not to be rude or anything, but… you got the cash?"

She smiled thinly as if she'd expected his question, opened her purse and pulled a small wad of bills free. "I believe this should be sufficient to get us off the ground?"

His eyes bugged. There had to be at least five grand in her hand! "Whoa, lady—" he snatched the cash and tucked it under his arm, glancing around "—don't go flashing that kind of money around here. Times are hard and you never know who's watching."

"You have a suspicious nature, Mr. Carmichael. I think that will serve my purposes quite well."

"Yeah? And what purposes would that be?"

"My own. When can we leave?"

"Look, I need to know some details. I can't just blindly agree to zip you off to South America just because you flashed some cash in my face."

"No? And why not?"

Uh… "Well, because I can't. How do I know you're not a drug dealer? I don't want to get caught up with the feds over some illegal shit."

"That's a pity," she said. "Because there's more where that came from if you could be trusted to do your job quietly and without question."

He didn't like her tone, but he had to admit she'd hooked him pretty good. "Yeah? Like how much?"

She smiled again. "Enough to make it worth your while."

Teagan's voice intruded in his thoughts, only this time J.T. had a feeling his brother was telling him to walk away because this job promised trouble. But that was a lot of cash. And cold hard cash was the answer to their prayers right now. He had no doubt that Blue Yonder could pull through if they could just weather this rough spot.

"When do you need to leave?"

"Now."

It was then he realized she'd come with a small rolling bag.

"Seriously?"

"As a heart attack." She glanced behind her before saying with a bit more urgency, "In fact, if we could be up in the air within the next ten minutes, that would be great."

Ten minutes? He had to file a flight plan, gain clearance… Hell, he had to drain his bladder and grab his meatball sub from the fridge. He chuckled, pumping the brakes. "Let's start with the basics. How about you tell me your name, where we're going, like a normal chartered excursion, and then we'll schedule your flight."

Her green-eyed gaze narrowed with irritation. "I don't have time for that. We need to be in the air *now*."

"Well, too bad. We have protocol, rules. I can't just go willy-nilly into the air like a drunken bird. I could lose my license."

"Mr. Carmichael…"

But whatever she was about to say was cut off by the sudden screech of tires.

"Shit," she muttered, her calm and precise demeanor crumbling quickly. "There's no time to argue. Let's go!"

A black car sped toward them, mindless of the tarmac, and J.T. got a real bad feeling. "What the hell?"

She shocked him by roughly pushing him. "We have to move, now! They are not coming this way to shake hands. Trust me—let's go!"

The way the car was barreling toward them, J.T. had to agree with the woman. Hell, he didn't even know her name yet, but there was no time for niceties. He grabbed her bag and tossed it into the cabin, then helped the woman in afterward.

"I hate when Teagan is right," he muttered, quickly buckling in and securing the cabin doors. He rushed through his preflight ritual—a quick prayer and a gentle swipe at the hula girl stuck to his cockpit dash—and gunned the engine. Taxiing, he hit the throttle and quickly picked up speed, but the distinct sound of bullets being fired put a whole new spin on things.

"They're shooting at my plane!"

"Yes, and if you don't get it in the air, we're going to end up in a fireball!"

"Who are you, lady?" he shouted, pushing forward on the throttle, his adrenaline running like jet fuel through his veins. "If anything happens to my plane—"

"Get us out of here alive and we'll talk! Until then, focus on getting us out of here!"

Couldn't argue that logic. J.T. wiped at the sweat gathering at his brow and pushed the plane to gain altitude. The sound of bullets hitting the frame was hard to ignore. He could just imagine the holes. Teagan was going to freak.

Resale value, J.T., he would no doubt yell. *No one's gonna want a shot-up plane!*

After what seemed an eternity, J.T. cleared the airfield and gained enough altitude to escape the trajectory of the bullets, but now that he was sure he wasn't going to die, he was pissed as hell!

If he'd wanted to be shot at he would've remained in the Air Force! He'd already done his share of tours in the combat zone and he was finished with that shit.

"You want to explain what the hell just happened?" he shouted. "Why are people shooting at you? Who are you? It's drugs, isn't it?"

"Yeah, actually, it is," she shot back, surprising him with her blunt answer.

He hadn't expected her to cop to it so easily. "Heroin? Meth? Pot?"

"Nothing illegal. Pharmaceuticals. I hate to burst your bubble, but what they're after is totally legal."

"Yeah, like I buy that," he shot back derisively. "Don't let my baby face fool you. I've been around the block enough times to know that people don't hand out bullet sandwiches for Tylenol. What the hell is really going on?"

"Look, nothing has changed. I'm still willing to pay an exorbitant amount of money for you to transport me to

South America. We've lost the people who were shooting at us, so let's just stay the course."

"Stay the course? Are you kidding me? People put bullets in my plane. There's no course I want to travel that involves bullets. You hear me? No way, lady. I'm finding the first open airfield and dropping you off. You can find a different chump to peddle your story to, because I ain't buying."

"No? From my research, Blue Yonder is dangerously close to shutting its doors. You're teetering on bankruptcy. I'm offering you one job that could put you in the black."

"How do you know my personal banking information?" he demanded, chafing at his privacy being invaded. He'd had enough of the government knowing his every move when he'd been property of the good ole US of A.

"Trust me—it's not as if you're living off the grid. A simple Google search with the right query and I found everything I needed to know. Am I right?"

"That's not the point," he groused, feeling exposed. "The point is, it's none of your business to go poking around in my private affairs."

"Look, I'm not the enemy. I'm just a scientist and I need your help to get to my company's lab in South America. Can you do that?"

"I can, but I won't," he answered, still thinking about the holes in his plane and how he was going to repair them when the bank account was dangerously dry.

She must've sensed a break in his resolve. "I can't express to you how important it is that I get to my destination. Make your offer and I'll pay it. My company will authorize a handsome sum to get what I'm carrying."

"What are you carrying?"

"Part of the deal will be no questions asked. It's safer for you that way."

"Well, now you're just leading me on. Either you tell me or I turn around."

"Your business will be toes up by next month," she countered firmly. "And then what? You have the opportunity to stave off the inevitable or maybe even pull out of this skid. But if you drop me off, your business is certain to fail because I didn't see anyone else knocking down your door to throw money at you."

He hated that she was right. Hadn't Teagan pounded that point into his head last night? Hadn't his brother's reasoning rung in his brain in spite of J.T.'s attempt to drown it out with Cuervo? By the bottom of the tequila bottle, things had seemed pretty hopeless.

Until the hot, troublesome redhead had walked onto the property.

But now he didn't know if he was about to make a devil's bargain.

"What kind of money are we talking?" he asked with grudging curiosity. He was already up in the air. Maybe it wouldn't be too much trouble to get her to where she needed to go, drop her off, then take the money and run.

"Enough to keep you afloat for a few months, maybe six if you're frugal. My company has very deep pockets."

Damn, that was persuasive. "And I'm just supposed to drop you off, no questions asked, and that's it? I never hear from you again and no more people come after me with guns?"

"That's exactly the deal, Mr. Carmichael."

Didn't seem so bad. Maybe it could work. It would certainly quell Teagan's all-fired desire to cut bait and bail on their dream.

He had to make a choice. They were about two minutes away from critical decision-making time. Giving up Blue Yonder was like asking him to cut off his favorite finger—the middle one—and he didn't see that happening. All they needed was a little time to sort things out. Business would pick up. He could feel it in his bones.

They flew past the last available airfield and his decision was effectively made.

"All right, I'll take the deal. But I need to know your name, at the very least, unless you want me to call you *Hey, lady* the entire flight."

"Seems fair enough." She took a breath and said, "My name is Dr. Hope Larsen. Pleased to meet you, Mr. Carmichael."

"Okay, let's get one thing straight… My father was Mr. Carmichael. If you know everything about my private business, but the color of my drawers, I think you can call me J.T."

She nodded. "J.T. it is, then."

"Doctor, huh? Like an MD?"

"Science doctor. A molecular biologist."

Damn. He knew the deal was to keep quiet, but the questions were already bubbling around in his head. What the hell kind of scientist got shot at? What was the pretty doctor involved with?

Collect the money and leave the questions.

That was sound advice—the kind of advice that would likely keep him on the right side of breathing.

But as he'd realized too late after one too many altercations with the higher-ups, he wasn't so good about taking orders without question.

He had a feeling dodging bullets might be easier than keeping his mouth shut.

As it turned out, they had bigger problems than the questions he wasn't allowed to ask.

"Shit," he muttered, his gaze trained on the altimeter.

"What's wrong?"

His lips seamed together. This was all sorts of bad.

"J.T.?" The worry in her tone mirrored the bad feeling in his gut. "Is something wrong?"

"Yeah, you could say that," he said, tapping his altimeter, hoping it was just a glitch. But when the needle continued to sink, he knew things were about to get dicey. His gaze traveled the gauges, locking on the fuel. *Bingo. You've located the problem.*

"What is it?"

"Buckle up, Doc," he said, gritting his teeth. "We're about to run out of gas."

"What?" She frantically tightened her belt. "Where are we?"

"Best guess? Somewhere over Mexico."

And nowhere near an airfield.

A grim smile found his mouth.

And he'd mistakenly thought getting shot at was the worst that could happen.

He just loved it when Murphy's Law seemed hell-bent on kicking him in the ass.

"WAIT! WHAT DO you mean you're running out of gas?" Hope screeched, unable to hide her panic. "Fix it. Do something!"

"I'm open to ideas, doll face, but unless you have a way to patch the hole that has no doubt been ripped through my fuel tank, we're out of options."

Sweat gathered at her brow as her fingers gripped the seat beneath her. "What are the odds of surviving a crash like this?" she asked, clinging to facts and figures as her life flashed before her eyes. "Give me a percentage."

"You don't want to know." His grim answer wasn't very soothing. He muttered expletives as he fought the throttle, and she squeezed her eyes shut, wishing at the moment that she'd been more religious. She supposed now was not a good time to question her decision to be an atheist.

The little plane hit a rough pocket and they dipped hard, causing a girlie scream to pop from her mouth. She thought of the package she was transporting and her panic doubled. "You have to promise me that if we crash and I die, you have to take the package that I'm carrying straight to Tessara Pharmaceuticals. Don't let anyone else take it from you. Promise me!"

He didn't have time to shoot her a look, but she could hear it in his voice as he yelled, "What the hell are you talking about, lady? I'm just trying to land safely and you're spitting out your last will and testament. Don't you know it's bad luck to talk about death when you're in a plane that's about to go down in a fireball? Just shut up, buckle up and let me try to save our damn lives!"

Hard to argue with that logic. Hope wasn't the kind of woman to scare easily, but it was hard to stay cool and collected when she was sitting in a metal coffin as it hurtled to the ground. Picking Blue Yonder had been a calculated risk. Right about now, she was rethinking that decision. Why hadn't she taken her chances with first class?

A brilliant canopy of verdant green rapidly approached the descending aircraft, and even though he'd told her to shut up so he could concentrate, scared babbling escaped her lips.

"I don't want to die in this plane. I don't want to die like this. Please, J.T.! Oh, my God!"

"Brace yourself—this ain't going to be pretty!"

The tops of the trees scraped along the belly of the plane, scoring the metal as they barreled through the air, hitting branches and sending leaves flying as the plane bounced and crashed through the thick jungle foliage. Birds took flight as they careened wildly, narrowly missing thick tree trunks as they crashed to their possible deaths.

Twisted metal screeched as a wing took a hard hit and

the plane listed to the side, and it was all Hope could do to hold on for dear life.

The small plane went nose-first through a small tree, spraying obliterated shards of wood everywhere as they blasted through the humid jungle floor, slamming into another tree big enough to stop their descent.

Blackness eclipsed her vision at the point of impact and then there was nothing.

Hope slowly stirred, her hand going to her head and finding it sticky. The copper scent of blood followed, and she groaned as she did a shaky assessment of her own body. She was alive. It was a damn miracle.

She unhooked her seat belt and her recovering senses immediately smelled fuel leaking. J.T. was slumped forward, not moving, and Hope bit back the fear as she reached across the seat to check for a pulse.

At the tentative touch of her fingertips to his neck, J.T. groaned, but didn't awaken.

Hope didn't have time to sag with relief. The situation was no less dire. The fuel tank was leaking and at any moment the plane could become a scorch mark on the jungle floor. She unhooked J.T.'s belt and gently pushed his head back to assess the damage. Potentially a concussion. He must've slammed his head pretty hard with the crash.

"J.T., we have to get out of this plane." She tapped his face lightly, cringing at the knowledge that someone with a head injury shouldn't be jostled, but in light of the situation, she had to take the risk. "The fuel tank is leaking. We have to go now! Wake up, J.T."

She slapped his face a little harder and he groaned, opening his eyes blearily. "What the..."

"We crashed. We're alive, but that might not be for long if we don't get out of this plane," she said, maneuvering around him and opening the pocket door with a hard shove, her own head pounding. She dropped to the soft jungle floor with her pack, the sounds of wild things echoing in the humid air, and nearly broke an ankle as her heel cracked in two.

"Stupid idea to wear these, anyway," she muttered, grabbing her bag and pulling her sneakers free. Thank God she always packed her running shoes. She tossed her useless heels and shoved her feet into her sneakers, grateful for small favors. Her rolling pack converted to a backpack, a feature she would've needed in South America—she'd read travel warnings about thieves snatching rolling luggage straight out of tourists' hands—and once again, she thanked her stars for that bit of wise decision making.

J.T. was still a little out of it, but he managed to climb out of his seat and half crawl to the pocket door, where he promptly slid out and landed with a grunt at her feet.

"I think I just cracked a rib," he groaned, looking like a brand-new calf trying to walk on wobbly legs.

Hope quickly slipped beneath his shoulder to steady him and he went down like a sack of potatoes.

"Don't you dare pass out on me," she muttered, but he was out. What was she supposed to do now? Put him over her shoulder and pack him out in a fireman hold? He slipped from her grasp and went straight to the ground in an unconscious heap.

She wiped at the sweat and blood trickling down her face and grabbed J.T.'s arms, pulling him inch by excruciating inch away from the wreckage. Shoulders screaming, Hope managed to pull his deadweight far enough away from the plane before she collapsed beside him, breathing hard.

Okay, now what?

She was in the middle of the Mexican jungle, her pilot was injured and she had no idea how the hell they were going to get out of there alive, much less reach the South American compound.

Hope bit her lip as a wave of helplessness swamped her. It wasn't like her to cry, but at the moment she wasn't going to begrudge herself a few tears, because let's face it…

They were screwed.

2

J.T. AWOKE TO the mother of all headaches—worse than any hangover he'd ever experienced. If he'd had a hammer handy, he would've buried it in his skull to stop the pain—but then he remembered that he was lucky to be alive.

He struggled to open his eyes, but when his vision finally cleared, he saw the leggy doctor curled up next to him in a leafy bed that he knew for a fact he hadn't put together.

He gingerly touched where his head throbbed and found a respectable goose egg where he must've smacked his nob on the control panel when they were going down. Best guess, mild concussion, which would explain why he'd passed out.

Hope stirred and she awoke, rubbing at her eyes as she sat up with a tired yawn, clearly relieved to see him still alive.

"Thank God," she breathed, her hands fluttering to her chest, where her formerly fancy cream blouse was now tattered and torn. "I was so worried you were going to die in the middle of the night."

"Ye of little faith," he grumbled, scooting to a sitting position, wincing as his head protested the small movement. "Takes more than a bump on the head to put me down. Trust me—others have tried."

"Well, tough guy, you've no doubt suffered a concussion, and if your brain had continued to swell, I would've been helpless to do anything about it."

"Lucky for me, I woke up just fine," he replied dryly, surveying their situation. Great, they were somewhere in the Mexican jungle. Deep. Which put them squarely between up a creek and wedged against a hard place. He rose to his feet, groaning without shame at the way his body screamed with pain. "Been a long time since I had to bring a plane down like that. It's as shitty as I remember."

"You've done this before?" Hope asked, rising to her feet as well, swiping at her behind as if that small motion were going to make a difference in the grime they were covered in. "You might've mentioned that before I chartered your service."

"Settle down, Doc. It was a long time ago, in another life," he said, scanning the jungle, looking for something that might tell him where they'd gone down. Thunderclouds rolled ominously on the horizon, temporarily blotting out the early sun. "My guess is that the plane didn't blow up?"

"No. I was afraid that it might, though, so I pulled you away from it."

Awww, she cares. "Thanks. I owe you one."

"Well, don't get the wrong idea. You're still on the clock, Mr. Carmichael. I need you to get me to South America."

"Lady, my plane is in pieces. How am I supposed to do that exactly? Put you on my back and flap my wings? We're going to have a bitch of a time getting out of this jungle alive, much less finding another plane to fly your happy ass to Timbuktu." He paused, then added, "And I told you, my father was Mr. Carmichael. It's J.T. or else I'm not answering."

"Fine. J.T. Here's the situation as I see it—we need each other to get out of this jam, so I suggest we work together instead of against one another so we can survive." She squared her shoulders and adjusted the fluttering sleeves of her mangled blouse and asked, "Do you have any idea where we might've landed?"

"Best guess? Somewhere in the Lacandon Jungle, likely the southern part of the Yucatán Peninsula." He bracketed his hips, squinting against the morning sun playing peek-aboo with the clouds. "And if that's the case, we're well and truly screwed."

"Why is that?"

"Well, because we have two possible situations and neither is good."

"Which are?" She gestured impatiently.

"First, we have the potential of running into Mexican guerrillas who are using the jungle reserve to grow their illegal crops and guard their crops with semiautomatic weapons and a 'shoot first, leave the body for the bugs' mentality, or second, we have the potential of running into the last Lacandon Maya, who don't interact with outside cultures and don't take kindly to strangers. I think they might even be cannibals, but don't quote me on it."

"That doesn't sound promising," she murmured in distress.

And since he didn't believe in sugarcoating things, he added, "Yeah, and that's not counting the bugs, snakes and apex predators that call this patch of earth home."

Hope paled and a bridge of soft brown freckles appeared on her nose. "I don't like snakes."

"Yeah, I don't either, but we did land in Satan's armpit, otherwise known as the Mexican rain forest."

"So what do we do?"

"Try not to die?"

Her mouth firmed with exasperation. "Obviously. What

about a road? There has to be something that eventually leads to civilization around here. It's not as if we fell onto an uninhabited planet. We'll just follow the river. That should lead somewhere."

"Yeah, right over a cliff. Look, the plane didn't blow, which means by this point it's not going to. I'll trek back to the plane, grab a few flares and other survival supplies, which, thankfully, include a compass and a map. We'll regroup after that."

"I'm going with you."

"No, you should stay here," he argued, but she wasn't going to budge. "Lady—"

"Stop calling me that. If I'm supposed to call you J.T., you can call me Hope. That's the deal. One more 'lady' or 'Doc' and I'm calling you Mr. Carmichael, and since you seem to have an aversion to that, I suggest you pay attention to what's falling from your mouth."

"You're a bossy bit of goods, you know that, *Hope*?"

She took that as a compliment. "A common enough label for a strong woman. I'll wear it with pride."

He barked a short laugh. "All right, fine. Let's get to the plane and see if we can't find our way out of this place."

They started making their way back to the plane, being mindful of their steps, when Hope asked, "So, why do you hate being called Mr. Carmichael? Did you have a tense relationship with your father?"

J.T. pushed away a large leafy branch and held it so she could pass. "You could say that. Me and the old man didn't see eye to eye on a lot of things. He thought I was a mouthy, disrespectful punk and I thought he was an overbearing, arrogant asshole."

"Were you?"

"Was I what?"

"A disrespectful punk."

"At times."

Hope glanced back at him. "Well, maybe he was an overbearing jerk because he was trying to provide some discipline to a kid who was, in his opinion, going down the wrong path."

"And maybe he was just a controlling closet alcoholic who cheated on every woman he ever tricked into loving him and at his core was a narcissistic waste of oxygen."

Way to go, J.T. Why don't you pull up a leaf and start spilling your whole life story while you're at it. "It doesn't matter what he was, anyway. The old man is dead to me and I'm done talking about it."

"I'm sorry. I didn't mean to touch a nerve."

Touch a nerve? She'd done more than touch it; she was standing on it. "You know, in the short time I've known you, I've been shot at, my plane crashed and now I'm pissed off about a man I haven't seen in eight years and haven't spared a thought for, either. If I didn't know better, I'd say you were bad luck."

She scoffed. "There's no such thing as luck."

"That's where you're wrong. Luck has kept me alive and you can thank your stars you hitched a ride on that luck because you're alive when that crash should've killed us both."

To illustrate that point, they broke the clearing where the plane had crashed and J.T. groaned at the damage. It wasn't as if he'd actually thought there was hope the plane could be fixed, but maybe, in the back of his mind, he'd clung to the irrational idea that it could be.

That is, until he saw the poor busted-up heap of metal.

"Damn," he breathed, rubbing the stubble on his jaw as he saw Blue Yonder's aspirations go up in smoke.

"I'll buy you a new plane," Hope said, hoping to soften the blow. When he cast her a dubious look, she added, "I told you, my company has deep pockets. Get me safely to South America and you can add the cost of your plane to the bill."

"Where the hell do you work?" he asked incredulously. "The Pentagon?"

Hope offered a short smile, but didn't answer. "Your flares?" she prompted.

Yeah, right. The more he found out about Hope, the less he actually knew.

And he had a feeling that wasn't going to change anytime soon.

Eye on the prize, Carmichael. Eye on the prize.

All he wanted was to get out alive.

WHILE J.T. GATHERED up the supplies from the fallen plane, Hope dug through her backpack to find some protein bars she'd stashed for the flight. She also found her cell phone, but, as expected, there was no service. However, she hoped that when she didn't show up at the designated point, her colleagues would start tracking its GPS.

She tucked the phone back into her pack and tried to repair her bedraggled blouse. There was no help for it— the top was ruined—so she gave up.

J.T. emerged from the wrecked cockpit with an Army-style pack of his own and dropped to the ground.

"I never thought I'd have to use this, but thank God Teagan made me keep one in the plane at all times." He lifted the pack and shouldered it. "The water-purifying tablets might save our bacon. You don't want to know what kind of bacteria swim around these parts."

"I'm a molecular biologist. Chances are I know more about the microbes and bacteria than you," she said with an enigmatic smile that J.T. found immediately inappropriately arresting and annoying. She was the prettiest know-it-all he'd ever come across, that was for sure. "What else is in your survival pack? I have some protein bars. That should help blunt the hunger pains for a while."

"It's no meatball sub, but it'll do," he said, wishing he'd been able to grab his sandwich before the bullets had started flying. *Good ole hindsight.* "Tarp and rope, which we're going to need if it—"

As if on cue, Mother Nature rumbled and a torrent of rain began falling from the sky, instantly drenching them both, forcing them to climb back into the plane to escape the deluge.

Dripping from head to toe, J.T. laughed at Hope's expression. "You look about as happy as a wet cat."

She shook the rain from her hands and removed her glasses as she wiped her face. "You called this place Satan's armpit?"

"Yeah."

"Fitting."

Thunder rumbled as a flash of lightning lit up the sky, and the rain pelted the metal frame of the plane, sounding like a barrage of gunfire.

Huddled in the downed plane, Hope sighed and broke into the protein bars, offering one to J.T. "Might as well have a bite while we wait out this storm," she offered.

J.T. accepted the chocolate bar and broke it in half, then handed her the other half. When she looked at him in question, he explained, "We should ration what we have for food. God only knows how long we'll be trekking through the jungle."

"Good point," she agreed, shuddering delicately, as the reality of their situation was hard to ignore. She stuffed the other bar back into her bag and slowly chewed her half of the protein bar.

He startled her when he reached across, brushing her belly as he leaned to grab something at her feet. "Excuse me?" she exclaimed at having her personal space invaded. "What are you doing?"

"Gotta take advantage of the water falling from the sky," he answered, lifting a canister and causing her to blush at her reaction. He fashioned a hook from some wire he had in a small toolbox and before long had the canister hanging out the pocket door, catching the rain. He grinned, saying, "No need to filter the rainwater. That way we can save our purifying tablets."

"Another good point," she murmured, shifting in the seat, wondering why she reacted so viscerally when J.T. was close. Of all the inappropriate times to notice that rugged physique and those tight, trim hips. A bit of protein bar snagged in her throat and she began to sputter. Horrified, she tried to swallow, but it seemed stuck.

"Here, drink," he instructed, pulling the canister inside to give it to her. "Talk about fortuitous. Or, as some might say, *lucky.*"

She closed her eyes and swallowed what water was in the canister, relieved that her throat had stopped spasming. "Thank you," she said, her voice ragged. Hope sagged against the worn leather of the seat and returned the canister so he could hang it out the door. When he returned to his seat, she added, "Still don't believe in luck."

J.T. shrugged, then settled in the seat, stretching his legs out as far as he could, which wasn't too far in the cramped cabin. "We have time to kill. Tell me why people are shooting at you."

"I already told you that it was better if you didn't know too many details."

"I don't usually tempt fate by asking what else could happen, but, really, we're staring down the business end of some really craptastic circumstances already, so what's the harm in telling me what you're running from?"

"I'm not running from anything," she said, frowning. "I told you, I work for a pharmaceutical company."

"Last time I checked, pharmaceutical companies didn't offer hazard pay because their researchers were going to have to dodge bullets. What's the real story?"

The real story? She was carrying, quite possibly, the most dangerous virus known to man in a special case in her pack and if she didn't reach the South American facility…well, a pandemic of the most devastating proportions could be the result.

Or if the virus fell into the wrong hands…

Hope shuddered to think.

And yes, the people who shouldn't have a biological weapon of this magnitude were the ones shooting at her.

"I don't want to talk about it," she said, her eyes welling with tears she hadn't allowed herself to shed until this moment. Tessara Pharm had their hands in so many pies, but this project had eclipsed everything else.

Her boss, Tanya Fields, was dead, and even though the police had deemed it a robbery gone wrong, the fact that Hope's house had been trashed the same night had sent her running.

Well, that and the fact that Tanya had suspected that someone within Tessara had sold proprietary secrets about the virus, which was why Tanya had entrusted Hope to destroy it.

"Hey, where'd you go?" J.T. asked.

Hope shook her head, not about to share. "I said I don't want to talk about it. I'd appreciate if you respected my privacy."

She didn't blame him for his questions, but she couldn't stomach the idea of another person dying because of this virus. Especially when, if things had been different… No, she wasn't going to go there. Dating had never been easy for her. She sucked at small talk because she saw little point and first dates were almost entirely comprised of the useless chitchat that she abhorred.

"I'm sorry," she apologized, attempting to be less prickly. "I don't mean to be rude. I'd just prefer—"

"That I keep my nose out of your business," he concluded, and she nodded. "Well, ordinarily, that's a rule I live by, but then, this is not your ordinary circumstance. If I'm being chased and shot at...I'd like to know what I might be eating a bullet for."

The thing was, Hope had this insane desire to actually tell J.T. everything, to just lay it all on the line and let him know exactly what they were up against, but that wasn't fair to him. The fact was, this was her burden. She'd helped create the virus; it was up to her to destroy it.

She sighed and said as she turned away to watch the rain through the murky window, "Just get me to South America and you never have to see me again."

3

THE RAIN FELL most of the afternoon, which afforded them the opportunity to catch some z's without fear of snakes or big cats dropping by for a snack, but J.T. knew they couldn't hole up in the plane forever.

He was already twitchy about being spotted by the guerrillas who hid out in these dense jungles, and it was better to be on the move than hanging around like a sitting duck.

While Hope slept, he climbed up into the cockpit and tried the radio, but it was deader than dead. All of the electronics were fried, which wasn't a huge surprise, but he wasn't above praying for a miracle.

Hope stirred, but didn't awaken, her glasses slipping down her nose a bit. Her red hair had escaped the elastic she'd managed to tie the massive red cloud with and she looked like a hot mess with her torn and tattered blouse and skirt.

And why did he find that incredibly arousing?

Of all the damn wrong times to get some wood going, this was it.

But his cock didn't care about circumstance—it just wanted what it wanted.

His stomach growled, protesting at the half protein bar

that'd long since left his gut, and he wondered what the hell he was going to do to get them out of there alive.

His Air Force training kicked in and he grabbed his map and compass. Granted, he'd never been this far south before—his Mexico trips had been liquor-soaked and of the party-resort type—but he knew enough about the terrain to know that if they were close enough to Guatemala, they could possibly find a small plane and hump it to Brazil within five hours.

The challenge would be making it out of the jungle first.

The second challenge would be finding a trustworthy local to procure a plane.

And the third challenge would be getting back in the air before the mystery shooters who had brought them down in the first place tried to finish the job.

What the hell was she packing that people were willing to kill to have?

He eyed the pack at her feet and gauged how deeply she was sleeping.

Maybe he'd just take a peek. Seemed fair to know what he was risking his life for, right?

Invasion of privacy, Teagan would warn, but J.T. pushed away his brother's voice. Some things were worth the risk.

But as he started to reach for the pack, her eyelids fluttered open and he casually shifted in his seat as if he'd been seeking a more comfortable position, and she was none the wiser.

"How long was I out?" she asked, rubbing at her eyes and yawning. Distress colored her voice as she looked out the window. "It's still raining? How long is it supposed to rain?"

"It's the rain forest, babe. It could rain for days."

"We have to get out of here," she protested, twisting in her seat to stretch her back. "Maybe we should just strike out and take our chances."

"Take our chances with the rain and everything else that's out there? No, thanks. We have to wait out the storm. Besides, it'll be night soon and you don't want to be traipsing around the jungle in the dark."

She seemed to realize the wisdom of his advice, but as she worried her lip, her gaze darting, he realized she might have a different sort of problem.

"You need to pee?"

Hope lifted her chin, determined to be an adult about things. "Yes." But her eyes darted again and her teeth returned to her lip. "But what about the jaguars and snakes and all those other things you mentioned?"

"Want me to stand guard?" he offered, to which she scowled. He lifted his hands in mock surrender. "Hey, just trying to help."

She climbed past him, then after gazing unhappily at the rain, climbed from the plane and disappeared. He chuckled at how ridiculous girls could be about that stuff, but remained mindful of how long she was gone. He might joke, but there were serious dangers lurking in the brush.

Hope reappeared quickly and climbed back inside, her blouse sticking to her skin in all the right places as she shook the water from her hair, and groaned as she sank into the seat.

"I can't sit in this plane for another ten hours. I'm going insane. I'm used to working fourteen-hour days with barely enough time to shove something down my throat before heading back to my lab. This is torture."

No, that smoking hot body is torture. It would be his bad karma to be holed up with a sexy scientist. What the hell was wrong with him? Maybe he'd hit his head harder than he'd realized.

During his tours with the Air Force, J.T. had learned how to shut off his brain for long stints, taking the opportunity to doze and conserve energy, which, once you got the hang of it, was rather Zen. Or, well, it was the closest he'd ever get to a Zen state of mind, that was for sure.

"Try to relax. We can't go anywhere, so we might as well save our energy," he said, closing his eyes.

"It's not in my personality to sit idle."

"There's always a first time for everything."

She huffed in annoyance. "Is there nothing that creates a sense of urgency for you?"

He opened his eyes to regard her thoughtfully, then answered, "Sure. A hot meatball sub, which, I might add, is chilling in my fridge as we speak. It was supposed to be my lunch."

"I'll add it to my tab," she quipped.

"You do that," he murmured. After a moment of strained silence, he reopened his eyes and asked out of sheer curiosity, "So…I take it there's no Mr. Doc Larsen waiting at home while you traipse around the country?"

Hope laughed awkwardly. "No, no husband at home. But if I did have a husband, he would be fully supportive of my work and my need to traipse about the country, as you put it. Most evolved men are supportive of their wives' career goals. Please don't tell me you're one of those guys who think women should be in the kitchen."

"Of course not. I support women picking up the tab at dinner. More power to them. Better for my cash flow, too."

She made a face. "That's not exactly what I meant."

"Oh, you mean you still want the guy to pick up the tab for dinner, but heaven help a man who holds a door open for you, right?"

"That's ridiculous. There's a difference between chivalry and being a male chauvinist."

"Look, I'm all for equality for men and women. Some of the best pilots I flew with were women. I'm just saying, there's nothing wrong with enjoying certain traditional gender roles. Such as…a woman cooking a nice meal for her man. You know what they say—the way to a man's heart is through his stomach."

"Then I'm out of luck. I can't cook to save my life."

"No?"

"Not a thing. I mean, I can heat up TV dinners, but for the most part I eat at the office cafeteria. They make a mean mac and cheese. It almost tastes like real cheese."

He grimaced. "That sounds disgusting."

She shrugged. "Food is fuel."

"No, food is more than fuel. Good food is like an orgasm for your mouth."

Hope gasped and blushed, immediately flustered. "Well, I don't look at it that way. Besides, I don't have time for…orgasmic food experiences."

J.T. liked seeing Hope blush. The sudden pinkening of her cheeks softened her face and made him think of other things that might make her blush.

He sighed dramatically. "That's a pity. You're missing out." And he left it at that with a slightly crooked grin.

The rain lightened to a steady drizzle as night fell. The jungle sounds seemed to amplify, and a sudden howling and screeching nearly startled Hope out of her chair.

"Probably howler monkey," he supplied to calm her nerves. "Harmless, but loud." But to be on the safe side, J.T. pulled in the water canister, closed the pocket door and latched it for the evening.

He took a swig and offered Hope the canister, which she accepted. After they'd drunk about half, he screwed the top back on and placed it in a safe spot, away from their feet, then closed his eyes.

"Are you going to sleep?" she asked.

"Sounded like a good idea."

"Okay."

He shot a quick glance at Hope as she tried to get comfortable in the leather chair. The plane wasn't in bad shape considering it'd dropped out of the sky and skidded to a stop on the jungle floor. They were lucky the cabin hadn't been ripped to pieces.

Again, there was that luck factor.

"Get some sleep. Tomorrow is going to be a bitch."

"That sounds promising," she grumbled.

He smiled grimly and closed his eyes.

Darling, you have no idea.

THE NEXT MORNING, Hope awoke ravenous with a full to bursting bladder. She maneuvered around J.T., who was still sleeping, mouth open slightly and gently snoring, to relieve herself and prayed fervently as she squatted that a snake would not think her derriere was a good place to sink its fangs.

Finished, she returned to the plane to find J.T. doing the same, only he hadn't felt the need to hide behind a tree.

She shouldn't stare.

But J.T. had the kind of body that females noticed—even if they were doing their best to ignore every muscled inch.

Hand bracing himself against the plane, pants slung low on his hips, he groaned with relief as he pissed on the ground.

Hope had just enough time to whirl around before J.T. turned and saw her gawking at his body.

"Oh, hey, sorry, I thought I could finish before you returned." He zipped and said, "All clear. No worries about seeing anything that might frighten you. I remember what you said about snakes."

Hope turned and faked a smile at his joke. "Very funny. As long as your snake doesn't bite, I'm sure I'll be fine."

J.T. guffawed and rubbed at the stubble on his beard. "Well, at least the rain has stopped, right? Gotta be thankful for small favors."

True enough, but even as she was anxious to get moving, she knew the trip wasn't going to be easy.

"Right. Let's eat our rations and pack up. I want to use as much daylight as we can before we have to stop and make camp." She rummaged in her pack and pulled out the last protein bar, breaking it in half so they could share it as they had before. "Bon appétit."

Hope made sure to really savor each pseudochocolaty bite in the hopes that her stomach realized it would have to go without for the rest of the day unless they happened upon a burger joint in the middle of the jungle that allowed you to pay with a credit card.

Within moments they were finished with their woefully inadequate breakfast/lunch/dinner ration and began to pack, but Hope had to keep stopping when the torn sleeves of her blouse kept snagging and getting in the way. "This stupid shirt…" she grumbled, wishing she'd chosen something more practical for the trip.

J.T. surprised her when he stepped over and ripped the sleeves plain off, untucked the blouse from her tattered skirt and tied the front in a knot tightly around her waist. "There, that ought to help," he said, grinning. "And it looks better, too."

Hope gaped, unable to believe what he'd just done. She glanced down at her ruined shirt and realized he was right. At least it wasn't going to get caught on branches now. Although she wasn't entirely comfortable with how much skin was showing, J.T. seemed fine with it.

Ahem, he seemed *more* than fine with it if the appreciative glimmer in his eyes told the truth.

"Thank you," she murmured, shouldering her pack and hoisting it higher on her back and tightening the straps.

The low buzz of an approaching aircraft caught their attention and Hope immediately started waving frantically to catch the pilot's attention. J.T. yelled, "Get down!" and tackled her to the ground to hide in the foliage.

"What are you doing?" she screeched, unable to believe he'd just submarined a possible way out of the jungle. "That could be our rescue plane!"

"I can guarantee that is not a rescue plane," he growled, holding her tight. "Remember how I said there were guerrillas in this jungle? Well, they use ultralight aircraft to patrol their territory, such as that Cessna that just flew overhead. Chances are they saw the plane down, which means they're going to circle back around for a better look. We gotta get out of here, now."

A flutter of alarm traveled her spinal cord. "What if they saw me?"

"Let's not hang around and find out," he said, letting her go as they climbed to their feet. The sound of the aircraft returning put their feet into sudden motion as they ran into the jungle, trying to lose themselves within the dense canopy.

Branches scraped her face and thick tree roots tripped her more than once as they ran like bats out of hell until they could no longer hear the plane, but by that point they were so deep in the jungle Hope was terrified that they'd gone from the frying pan to the fire.

Breathing hard, sweat running down their faces, they stopped to catch their breath as they regrouped.

"Do you think they saw us?" she asked when she could speak again.

"No way to know," he answered grimly, and drew a deep breath. "But we gotta keep moving."

"But we don't even know where we're going!" she protested. "We could be heading in the wrong direction."

"We'll follow the river. At least we'll have access to drinking water."

"But you said the river would take us over a cliff," she reminded him anxiously.

"I guess we'll just have to be careful."

He flashed her a grin that belied the seriousness of the situation and she couldn't help but feel a tiny bit reassured that they were going to be all right.

As long as they weren't eaten.

Or shot.

4

J.T. TOOK POINT, pushing through the dense jungle, getting slapped and scratched by branches, as they slipped on slick mud and swatted at the mosquitoes that buzzed around their heads. By the time they reached the river bend, they were both hot, sweaty and hungry.

"That protein bar didn't go very far," Hope said, squinting at the midday sun, breathless. "I feel like my stomach is caving in."

"Same," he agreed, looking around. He knew that the Lacandon had plenty of edible fruits, tubers and greens, but he wasn't about to take a chance and gnaw on a leaf he couldn't identify.

And seeing as he wasn't a botanist, he couldn't identify much of anything.

However, Hope had better luck.

"Oh!" she exclaimed, moving past him to crouch on the jungle floor beside a leafy green bush that looked, frankly, exactly the same as the rest of the jungle, but when she rose with a triumphant smile and a handful of green pods, he knew she'd found something. "These are edible berries," she explained, plucking the green buds and pouring a few into his palm.

"Are you sure?" he asked, regarding the buds with uncertainty. "I don't want to die hallucinating that the Stay Puft Marshmallow Man is coming to eat me."

"They are completely safe," she assured him, popping her handful into her mouth. Immediately grimacing, she added, "But no promises on how they taste. Good gravy, that's a different flavor altogether."

He followed suit and experimentally chewed on the berries. "Whoa, you aren't kidding," he said, trying to categorize the flavor. "Not sweet, a bit sour…and grainy."

She nodded and swallowed. "But edible. We should eat a few more."

"I'm not sure starving wouldn't be preferable to putting those things in my mouth again, but I'll take your word for it." He accepted a few more round green buds and hastily tossed them back, chewing quickly so he could get it over with. "What I wouldn't do for my meatball sub," he groused.

Hope commiserated, swallowing quickly. "Never been a huge fan, but right now I'd go face-first into that sub if it were in your hands."

J.T. laughed and pulled the water canteen to wash down the jungle gunk. "Here, take a few swigs. The aftertaste is a killer."

They shared a few drinks and then surveyed their situation. "Best guess, this is the Lacanjá River. If we follow it, we should run into a few villages. With any luck, we can hitch a ride to one of the bigger cities closer to Guatemala or Belize. From there we can regroup and find another plane."

"And what if this isn't the Lacanjá River, but some other tributary and we end up more lost than ever?"

"Then we're going to be eating a lot more of those disgusting berries," he said grimly. But, God, he hoped it wouldn't come to that.

"That's not a great prospect," she said.

"Tell me about it."

They wound their way along the river's edge, slipping and sliding, landing more than once in the water, before they realized they were running out of traversable land and would have to double back.

"Maybe we could let the current take us downriver," Hope suggested, and bit her lip in distress. Thinking better of her own suggestion, she said, "Or we could just find an alternate route."

"The current is moving pretty fast. I wouldn't want to take the chance if we didn't have to."

Hope agreed, sighing heavily. As they turned to go back the way they'd come, they heard the distinct sound of voices speaking Spanish heading their way and froze.

"What do we do?" Hope asked fearfully, swallowing as she stood rigid. "They're going to see us any second!"

J.T. did some quick thinking and came up with two possible scenarios. Stick around and die, or jump in the water and possibly drown—only one option had a slim shot of survival. Grabbing her hand, he yelled, "Jump!" right as a bullet split the air by his ear and they went feetfirst into the fast-moving river.

If he hadn't been choking on river water, the sudden cool of the water would've been refreshing, but the brutal current was tossing them around like rag dolls, pulling them under as they went, only to spit them out again as they drew quick lungfuls of precious air.

"J.T.!" Hope managed to scream before going under again. He swam toward her and managed to grab her hand and pull her to him, but the waves buffeted them, doing their best to tear them apart.

"Don't let go!" he yelled, gripping her hand so hard he would've feared under normal circumstances that he'd snap bone.

J.T. popped out of the water in time to see the worst-case scenario materialize before his eyes. *Awww, shit.* A waterfall loomed and they were heading straight for it.

He knew they had seconds before they went over, so he used the time to shout quick instructions.

"Whatever you do, try to go feetfirst into the water. With any luck…we won't hit rocks!"

"Rocks?" she cried, ending with a shrill, *"OHHMYY-GOD"* as they plunged over the side.

It would be a miracle if they survived.

And J.T. worried…they might be plain out of miracles.

Hope surged to the surface with a huge gasp as her lungs screamed for air. Mist from the waterfall sprayed her face as she tread water looking frantically for J.T.

Oh, God, please don't be dead. "J.T.?" she called out, desperately hoping that some kind of luck—even if she didn't believe in luck—was on their side.

J.T. popped up from beneath the water and she nearly cried with relief. She swam to him and immediately went into his arms, so grateful that he was alive that she didn't care that he was a relative stranger. Immediately aware of the strength rippling in his arms as he held her afloat, she found herself a little breathless.

"You okay?" he asked, and all she could do was nod gratefully.

"You're alive," she said, smiling through tears that had suddenly appeared without warning. "I thought you were dead when you didn't surface right away."

"More weight…went deeper," he grunted, his arms tightening around her, water spraying all around them.

"I was scared," she admitted, pushing away the wet hair clinging to her face. "I thought for sure we were both dead."

"Not dead yet," he said with a ragged smile, showing no signs of letting her go, and she was okay with that.

More than okay.

Was it bad that she wanted to wrap herself around him and never let go?

Of course it was.

"Well, glad you didn't die," Hope said, reluctantly pulling away so she could gather her wits before they floated away along with her self-respect.

"That makes two of us," he said from behind her as they swam away from the falls to climb onto the rocks lining the bank of the river.

Hope cautiously stood on a slippery flat rock to survey where they'd landed.

"It's like something off a postcard," Hope noted with wry amusement at the raw natural beauty of the scenic lagoon as her gaze traveled up the waterfall. She shuddered at how high they'd fallen. Had she really just gone over the falls like a skipping stone? She didn't even like staying on the top floors of hotels! "But I never want to do that again."

J.T. paused in shaking his head like a shaggy dog to squint up at the falls. "Yeah, that was an adrenaline rush, wasn't it? Reminded me of the time I went bungee jumping off the Royal Gorge Bridge in Colorado. I thought I was going to piss myself. It was great."

"I don't understand the fascination people have with putting themselves in terrifying situations simply for the biochemical response created by saturating your brain with fear hormones."

J.T. shrugged as if he'd never taken the time to ask the question, nor did he care. "It was fun. We went out for beers afterward. Good times." He eyed her with interest. "You mean to tell me you've never done something simply for the thrill factor?"

"My idea of a thrill does not involve the potential of

bodily injury." Hope made her way gingerly from the rocks toward the bank. Turning to watch him as he followed, and trying to keep from staring at his perfectly molded physique, she added, "Besides, I find scientific discovery thrilling. You may not realize this, but a lab can be filled with excitement."

He laughed at her claim, but when she cast him a sharp look, he held up his hands in mock surrender. "I'll take your word for it." He maneuvered around her, holding his hand out to help her navigate the final rock.

Hope slipped and he yanked her into his arms before she could land on her behind. Sheltered in the warm cove of his arms, Hope had a hard time remembering why it wasn't completely natural to be cozied up to J.T. as if they were a newlywed couple enjoying an exotic honeymoon.

"Thank you," she murmured, intensely aware of how wonderful it felt to be pressed against all that solid muscle and just how long it'd been since she'd enjoyed the company of the opposite sex.

Hope gazed up at him, unable to break eye contact, even though she knew she should. "Extreme situations often cause an emotional response to the opposite sex that could be misconstrued as attraction," she explained, not only for his benefit, but for her own.

One dark eyebrow went up. "Are you feeling a misplaced attraction, Dr. Larsen?"

God, yes. "N-no, I was just saying…in case you're feeling something…that it could be a false notion."

"Thank you. I'll keep that in mind."

"You can let me go now." *But please don't.* Heaven help her, she wanted to do something reckless. Maybe it was the whole falling-off-a-cliff thing that was messing with her head, but it was really hard to ignore the overwhelming urge to seal her lips to his, if only to celebrate that they'd freaking survived what should've killed them.

"Those guys were shooting at us," Hope said, shuddering. "If we hadn't jumped…"

"Yeah, best not to think about that. Besides, we made it. Let's not look a gift horse in the mouth."

"Good idea."

Their lips were inches away from touching. It would be so easy to close the distance. His arms felt warm and secure tucked around her, their bodies fitting together almost perfectly.

"You're a good guy to have around in a crisis," she murmured.

"And you bring trouble," he countered with a sexy grin. "Good thing I like that about you."

Don't kiss him. Don't confuse the adrenaline of the moment with an inappropriate attraction.

The advice was solid, but it took a superhuman effort to disengage her hold around his neck and step away. Leaving the comforting feel of his solid body immediately made her feel vulnerable.

"What kind of snakes are in Mexico? Water snakes? Venomous? Constrictors?" she worried, scanning the dense foliage and the ground for anything that resembled a snake. "That's all I need, a snake bite to go with this already harrowing experience."

"I see your precious cargo made the fall, too," J.T. noted.

She double-checked her bag, breathing a secret sigh of relief when she confirmed that the special carrying case was still locked safely and securely. He frowned as he said, "You know, you could've drowned with that thing weighing you down. What's so special about that cargo that you're willing to die for it?"

Hope forced a light laugh. "No, no, a deal is a deal. No questions."

But he wasn't laughing.

"That was before I was shot at, my plane was ruined

and I went over a cliff with nothing more than a prayer. What the hell are you carrying around?"

Take a chance. Tell him. But even as she opened her mouth with the thought, Hope stuffed down the impulse, dismissing it as stupidly reckless—more so than kissing J.T. would've been—and switched gears.

She shouldered her pack and offered a sunny smile. "Nope. Best you don't know. Now, can we get moving? Daylight is wasting."

"That answer is getting real old," he growled, running his hands over his head, sending droplets everywhere. "You're a stubborn thing, you know that?"

"Haven't you ever heard the saying 'Well-behaved women rarely make history'?" she shot back coyly, yet her insides trembled with her need to come clean with J.T. *Just get the job done. Deliver the virus.* Those were the priorities. What did it matter what her hot pilot thought of her? "And yes, I am stubborn. I think it's one of my best qualities."

His gaze snagged on her chest area before bouncing away as if scalded. She gasped when she realized how completely see-through her blouse had become. She might as well have been naked. "Oh, goodness," she murmured, embarrassed. "I didn't realize…"

"I didn't take you for a pink-hearts kind of girl," he teased gruffly, referencing the tiny hearts that dotted the dainty white bra beneath her blouse.

"Yeah? Why is that?" she asked, laughing past her embarrassment. Would he be shocked to know her panties matched? "You think smart girls don't like to feel pretty?"

"I wouldn't know. I don't make a habit of shacking up with smart girls," he admitted with a shrug that was sexy as hell even if his quip did send her internal feminist into a tizzy.

"Which begs the question…what do you have against smart girls?"

"I don't have anything against smart women," he said, clarifying. "I try to avoid smart and *beautiful*. Seems a dangerous combination. And complicated."

"Only for a man who isn't secure enough to handle being with one."

J.T. staggered as if he'd been shot. "Ouch. You got me."

"Not that I care what your preferences are," she said, needing to make that clear, not only for J.T., but for herself. "I'm just making an observation."

"I'll take that under advisement," he said. "Anything else you want to get off your chest?"

The word *chest* made her think *breast* and reminded her of how J.T. had caught an eyeful, and her nipples pearled when her mind wandered to things best left alone.

J.T., the opportunist, laughed, his green eyes twinkling. "Catch a breeze?"

Hope scowled and started climbing the short bank, needing space between herself and J.T. She could still hear his quiet chuckling from behind her, but before she could whirl around and remind him of their professional relationship, her gaze caught the most beautiful sight in all the jungle—a road!

Embarrassment forgotten, Hope pointed, exclaiming, "There's a road up ahead. Do you think it's safe to follow?"

He didn't have a definitive answer, but they didn't have much choice. They both knew they couldn't hole up in the jungle for much longer. "We'll just have to take our chances," he said, taking point.

"That sounds dicey," Hope said, but she agreed it was a risk they had to take. "Here's hoping we're not hopping from the frying pan to the fire."

The road wasn't exactly maintained by modern standards. In fact, it seemed more of a suggestion than an actual roadway, but at the very least they weren't fighting jungle branches and slipping in mud up to their knees with every other step, and for that she was grateful.

Bare-chested brown children with shaved dark heads, wearing threadbare cotton shorts, stopped their play to smile shyly at the strangers who had shown up unannounced while the adults assessed them.

The fact that the locals wore Westernized clothing was the one small clue that they weren't in the most remote village in the Lacandon and that gave her hope. Well, that and the fact that there was an actual road running alongside the village. She'd never been so happy to see asphalt.

"Does anyone speak English?" J.T. asked, looking for anyone who might be willing to serve as a guide. "Anyone?"

Murmurs rippled through the group as they each turned to one another. Then they motioned a young man to come forward.

"We need a guide to get us back to a city with an airport," Hope said, offering a friendly smile. "We can compensate anyone who offers to help."

J.T. shot Hope a quelling look that warned, *Don't go mentioning money in a place where 80 percent of the population live well beneath the poverty line and eat dirt cookies for breakfast*, but she knew offering something of value was the only way they'd get them to budge.

A young teen with an oily shock of black hair hanging in his face spoke up. "I speak English," he said, pushing his hair from his dark eyes. "There's an airport in Comitán, about a four-hour drive from here."

"What village is this?" J.T. asked.

"Lacanjá."

"Lacanjá," Hope murmured, looking to J.T. "So we are on the southern edge of Mexico, near Guatemala?"

"Fair assumption."

"What's your name?" Hope asked the young man.

"Juan," the teen answered. "Welcome to our village. Are you hungry or thirsty?"

"Starved," Hope answered, her stomach grumbling. "Is there someplace we could get something to eat?"

"*Sí*, Campamento Vicente Paniagua—you will like."

"Sounds good to me," Hope said, looking for confirmation from J.T. When he gave her a short nod, she fell in line behind Juan, so grateful to be heading someplace somewhat civilized.

Maybe if they were lucky, they could be back in the air and back on schedule by tomorrow morning.

And then she could shelve these intrusive thoughts of hard pecs, solid thighs and the feeling of J.T.'s arms wrapped around her.

5

To HIS SURPRISE and Hope's delight, Campamento Vicente Paniagua was a nice little place that actually catered to ecotourists eager to experience something a little more adventurous yet still retain the comforts of home, such as running water and toilets.

And they took credit cards, which was a huge relief, as he hadn't exactly been able to grab his wallet before the mad dash to avoid getting killed and Hope immediately pulled out her company American Express.

"You ain't kidding about the deep pockets," he said, gesturing to the black American Express card. "Not many companies hand those out to their employees."

"I'm not just any employee."

"I gathered that." He dug into his plate of black beans and rice, never so happy in his life to stuff his mouth with the simple staple, but that first bite was nothing short of exquisite. Hope did the same, actually groaning with pleasure as she chewed. At the sound, J.T.'s overactive imagination was only too happy to supply alternate ways to make her moan. *Cut it out, Carmichael. Eat your beans. And whatever you do, don't dwell on the fact that you haven't stopped thinking about that damn pink-heart bra covering those sweet breasts.*

He actually choked a little, attracting Hope's attention, but he betrayed nothing that would give away the thoughts running like dirty monkeys through his mind.

"Juan said it will take a day to find a truck to take us to Comitán, but in the meantime we can stay at the Ecolodge. He assured us that the accommodations are very good. I told him as long as it has a bed and a bathroom, I'm grateful."

"Now that we're not jumping off cliffs and dodging bullets, I can take a moment to appreciate the natural beauty of this place," she said, as if they were just vacationing Americans.

Juan reappeared with an eager-to-please grin and gestured to them. "Your room is ready," he said, adding helpfully, "Honeymoon suite."

"Oh!" Hope's eyes widened, immediately looking to J.T. for backup, but he was actually glad for the single room. Although the risk was smaller with an obviously tourism-oriented village, he figured there was safety in numbers. Particularly for a beautiful redhead with legs for days.

The harsh truth was that human trafficking was alive and well in Mexico, and the sexy scientist would certainly turn heads.

"That'll be fine," he said, shocking Hope with his agreement.

"What are you doing?" she whispered. "I think I can afford to spring for two rooms."

"That's not the point. Safety in numbers. We're not in Idaho."

His meaning sank in and Hope nodded with dawning understanding. "That'll be very nice, Juan," she said, giving him a few American dollars from her pack. "Please show us to our room. I'm ready for a bath and a soft bed."

Juan led them to the Ecolodge and J.T. was suitably impressed with how clean and resort-like the accommodations were. *Thank God for Americans' need for comfort.*

They walked into the honeymoon suite and immediately they both centered on the huge bed dominating the room with the gauzy mosquito net draped over it.

It was Hope who spoke first. "We're adults. I think we're capable of sharing a bed without dissolving into teenage fits of giggles and awkward silence," she said, though he got the distinct impression she wasn't saying it for only his benefit.

"All I've got on my mind is sleep," he drawled with practiced nonchalance, but couldn't help but add with a cheeky grin, "However, I'm not opposed to cuddling."

Hope immediately scowled even as her cheeks flushed. "There will be *no* cuddling," she told him. "We need to keep things professional."

"Do you always live your life by so many rules?" he asked, curious to get a peek inside that brainy head of hers. "Or do you ever do anything a little off the rails for fun?"

"I have plenty of fun," she retorted stiffly. "I just don't see the value in muddying a business relationship with momentary pleasure. That's the problem with people today—they immediately jump into bed with someone before considering the full consequence."

"Sometimes you just have to go with the moment," he said with a shrug. "See where it'll take you."

"I know exactly where it'll take me," she said with a disapproving stare that could rival a Catholic-school nun's. "Which is exactly why I'm not going to succumb to something as ephemeral as what can be perceived as attraction."

"There you go throwing around scientific facts again. I don't care what your lab partners have told you—that ain't sexy."

"Good." Hope firmed her lips as if she didn't want to

explain herself, but prepared to do so, anyway. "Shared intense experiences can create a false sense of attraction that is often misconstrued as something deeper," she said, lifting her chin.

"So you keep saying," he said. "Care to put your theory to the test?"

Now why'd you go and poke the bear? The reasonable section of his brain was reminding him that pushing the sexy scientist beyond her comfort zone was a bad idea. But he rarely listened to anything coming out of that part of his brain, so why start now?

Maybe it was a shorted-out fuse or maybe it was the circumstance, but Hope, standing there, chin lifted, eyes flashing and damp hair still dripping, was doing something dirty to his thought process.

She'd felt pretty damn perfect in his arms under the waterfall. Every rounded curve and soft valley had pressed nicely against everything that was hard on him, and he was hungry for a little more of that sassy redhead.

And he didn't really care what was prompting it.

Be it science or otherwise.

"Wh-what are you doing?" she stammered, her eyes widening as he walked slowly toward her. Backing away, she tried protesting, "And it's not a theory—it's a proven scientific fact. Adrenaline can create a false attraction that's difficult to—" She stopped abruptly when her back hit the wall and a tiny gasp escaped her mouth.

"So prove it," he said in a low tone, trapping her within the space of his arms. "Has anyone ever told you that you're adorable when you're speechless?" J.T. brushed a kiss across her slightly open lips. "And damn near irresistible?"

"Wh-why are you doing this?" she managed to ask in a breathy tone that was more anticipatory than frightened and made his groin tighten. "We agreed to keep things professional."

"Yes, but as you can plainly see, things have changed significantly since we struck that bargain. And now it might be time to renegotiate."

He knew he ought to knock it off, and in truth, he'd started this just to mess with her, but now that he was in her space, he had lust rockets going off in his brain and he wasn't ready to stop.

"And what makes you think I'm open to negotiating?" she asked, trembling, her chin lifting.

"Darlin', if you don't stop looking at me like I'm your next meal, all that we'll be negotiating is where we're going to seal the deal," he said, unable to stop from leaning in, tasting her lips, wanting more. She groaned and opened her mouth to him, which was like tossing gasoline on a spark. Their tongues tangled and danced, sliding against each another. He slid his hands down to grab her wrists and pinned them to the wall, holding her in place as he continued to plunder her mouth.

She gasped against his mouth when he wedged his knee between her thighs, putting pressure on her mound, and the heat against his leg was enough to set him on fire.

"This isn't real," Hope groaned.

"Feels pretty real to me," he growled against her mouth as he pulled her away from the wall, loving how her eyes were glazed and her hair was wild. She looked like a B-movie warrior princess with all that gorgeous red hair and those sweet curves, and he couldn't wait to start their own version of an X-rated flick.

Her pupils dilated and her tongue darted as she began to breathe heavily, unable to disagree. "These things can be…hard to tell the difference…" she managed to say, but the look in her eyes told a different story.

He walked her to the bed, his gaze never leaving hers, and when she didn't protest or try to stop him, he didn't hesitate to claim what he shouldn't. His entire body was taut with need. He'd never felt so desperate to be inside a woman in his life. His hands shook as he lifted her skirt over her hips and laid her on the bed, sucking in a tight breath.

Sweet heaven...

Tiny pink hearts that matched her bra danced across her pubic mound and he couldn't help himself. Lifting her to his lips, he kissed each heart, inhaling the sweet musk of her feminine folds, teasing her through the thin fabric of her panties until she was groaning and lifting her hips higher with desperate mewls of frustration.

J.T. knew how to tease a woman until she was crying out, desperate for his cock, but it was hard to remember all his practice-made-perfect skills with Hope. There was something about her that made him feel like an inexperienced teen, fumbling around, blind as a bat and just as clueless as to what to do with a woman.

He groaned as the heavy ache in his balls intensified, the lust pounding his brain obliterating any rational thought. As much as he'd love to think he could spend the next hour teasing Hope with his tongue, his own impatience to taste her, to know her unique flavor, shoved any sexual finesse right out the door.

Ripping her panties off, he gazed at her sweet core, wet with desire, and he wasted no time in sinking between her legs to feast on that tasty jewel.

Hope cried out, her hands clutching at the thin bedspread as her legs quivered, her belly trembling as she succumbed with a gasp that turned him on more than he'd ever thought possible.

"Oh, my God," she whimpered when she could breathe again.

But that was just the appetizer and he was ready for the main course.

HOPE COULDN'T FOCUS. How could one orgasm zap her brain like an EMP blast? She'd heard stories of women who had such powerful orgasms that they were left stupid afterward, but she'd never truly believed them.

She was a believer now!

Good gravy, she was a believer.

J.T. slowly unzipped his jeans and the thick shaft of his cock was outlined in his boxer briefs, causing her mouth to water. She wanted to taste him as he'd tasted her.

But the look in his eyes was the thing that really caused her bones to melt. Never in her life had anyone looked at her that way—as if she were the most desirable, most beautiful, most intoxicating woman he'd ever seen.

And in that moment, she would've given him anything.

She rolled to her belly and slowly rose up on her knees, glancing coyly over her shoulder as he gazed hungrily, his hands reaching for her ass to squeeze the firm flesh.

"Like what you see?" she teased, which only intensified the heat between them.

"You have no idea," he returned, his voice tight and incredibly sexy, like everything else about the man. He gripped her hips and pulled her to him with one sharp movement, popping a gasp from her lips as he wasted no time in sinking into her body, plunging deep inside, going straight to the hilt, filling her completely.

Helpless to escape the mounting pressure building inside her, Hope gasped against the insane, mindless pleasure as J.T. continued to plunge inside her, over and over, wild and insatiable.

There was nothing but heat between them. Raging, inescapable, totally destructive fire.

And she gladly surrendered to every lick of the flame.

Blinding stars exploded in her brain as every muscle contracted in unison, tensing to the point of delicious pain, and she knew this kind of pleasure could be addicting.

J.T. was the kind of guy who could twist a woman in a pretzel with his sexual prowess, but would leave her crying in the end.

But at that moment, she didn't care.

The feel of J.T. filling her, stretching her, demanding everything she had and more…it was intoxicating.

She barely registered J.T.'s shout as he came, his thrusts becoming fierce and erratic as he poured himself into her until they both collapsed, breathing hard and unable to speak for several minutes.

Hope rolled to her back, staring unseeing at the gauzy mosquito netting. "That was…not natural."

J.T. laughed and rose to his elbow to regard her with a smile in his eyes. "Should I take that as a compliment?"

"I'm not sure."

"At least you're honest."

She exhaled a pent-up breath and tried to slow her heart rate. What happened now? How were they supposed to go back to being professional when they'd just rocked each other's socks off?

"You're overthinking things," he told her, smoothing the sudden wrinkle in her brow as the questions started to come at her from all angles. "It's just sex."

Hope rose and scooted away from him, needing space to think. "Of course it's just sex," she said, her voice a little high to be believable. "I'm fully aware of that. I just… Well, I don't make a habit of sleeping with random guys for the sake of *just having sex.*"

His smile faltered and he voiced a sudden concern that

should've been addressed before their clothes had flown off. "Please tell me you're on birth control…"

"Why is it always the woman who has to think of these things?" she shot back, irritated, not at his question, because it was a fair question, but because she hadn't had the self-control to ignore the white-hot attraction between them, whether it was induced by their circumstances or not. "And yes, I'm on birth control, so you can stop panicking."

"Thank God."

Hope sent him a short glare and scooted off the bed. She needed a shower and time to get her head on straight.

"Where are you going?" he asked.

"I need a minute to figure things out."

"What's to figure out? Why overthink things?"

She faced him. "That's your problem, J.T. You don't stop to think about anything. You're impulsive and reckless, but I'm not. I think things through. I look before I leap. I make pros-and-cons lists for every major decision and this thing that just happened between us is not part of my carefully orchestrated plan."

"Well, honey, sometimes life doesn't play out the way we want," he said, glaring. "Sometimes being impulsive and reckless, as you put it, opens up our world to a whole new array of possibilities that we never would've seen if we hadn't been forced to look around."

Hope didn't know why she was so out of sorts. It wasn't the first time she'd had sex with someone outside a relationship. Contrary to what was spilling from her mouth, she'd had one-night stands—not many, though—and walked away without an ounce of shame afterward.

But there was something about J.T. that put her off her game, sent her spiraling off-kilter, and it scared her.

It scared her more than the fact that someone was trying to steal her work and potentially threaten the entire human race.

Yeah, Hope. You've got your priorities straight.

She stomped her foot in agitation with herself, but glared at J.T. because she couldn't think of what else to do, and then slammed the bathroom door shut behind her.

Mature. Real mature.

Hope leaned against the bathroom door, embarrassed and unsure of how to handle herself.

So how were they supposed to sleep next to each other now?

6

J.T. LISTENED TO the sound of the shower on the other side of the thin door and tried not to fixate on the desire to join Hope.

Maybe in hindsight it wasn't a smart idea to sleep with your client.

He could just hear his brother lecturing him already. *For Christ's sake, keep your dick in your pants!* Or something along those lines.

And Teagan would be right, of course.

Because Teagan didn't make stupid decisions the way J.T. did on a regular basis.

Teagan didn't drop the ball and forget to file flight plans.

Teagan didn't spend his rent money on strippers and booze.

Teagan didn't risk everything on a gut feeling, willing to put everything on the line for a dream that refused to die.

Awww, hell, Teagan didn't need a screwup like him always making the wrong decision.

Speaking of...he had to find a phone so he could call his brother and let him know what'd happened.

By now Teagan would have discovered that the plane

had gone down and he was probably organizing a search-and-rescue op with some of his military contacts.

Finding a phone was a welcome distraction from the thoughts hounding him, and when he finally managed to talk the lodge manager into letting him make a collect call, he was relieved to hear Teagan's voice on the line.

"Where the hell are you?" Teagan asked, his voice bordering on a shout. "I came back to the hangar and found it shot to hell and the plane was gone. What happened?"

"It's a long story, bro, and when I get back to the States, I promise I'll tell you everything, but for now I just wanted to let you know I was okay and not to worry."

"Where are you?"

"Lacanjá, Mexico. The plane went down in the jungle. We barely survived."

"The plane went down?"

"Yeah, it's totaled."

Teagan swore under his breath, but what could he say that wouldn't make him sound as if he was being a total asshole in light of the fact that J.T. had almost died, right? "Look, go ahead and read me the riot act for screwing up again, but I thought this was going to be an easy enough job and it paid well enough to look past the obvious danger signs."

"What kind of danger signs?"

"Like people shooting at us."

"Us?"

"Yeah, me and the client, a woman by the name of Dr. Hope Larsen. She's some top scientist with a pharm corp that I've never heard of. She's promising to buy us a new plane if I can just get her to South America."

"A new plane?" Teagan repeated incredulously. "Did you get that in writing?"

"I think she's good for it. Hell, she's using a black American Express card for expenses."

"That's a good sign," Teagan allowed grudgingly. "You okay?"

"Yeah, banged up and bruised, but nothing a cold beer won't cure."

A beat passed and Teagan said, "Hey, I'm glad you're all right. Screw the plane. Just come home safe."

J.T. swallowed the lump that rose. In another life, he and his brother were Air Force pilots. Each time they went up in the air, they'd tell each other, "Just come home safe."

It'd been a long time since his brother had said those words to him.

Owning a struggling business together had put a strain on their relationship, one he hated.

That was why he'd taken Hope's offer. The opportunity to save Blue Yonder had been too tempting to pass up.

"Yeah, you know me…always operating on a wing and a prayer," he quipped, clearing his throat of the emotion choking him. "Look, I need a favor. We're heading to Comitán to pick up a new plane. Got any connections I can use to make that happen?"

"Hell, it's not exactly friendly territory," Teagan groused. "How can I reach you?"

"I'll work on getting a phone down here. I'll contact you when I do."

"I'll see what I can do about getting you a plane."

"Thanks, bro. I owe you."

"Just don't get yourself killed."

He grinned and clicked off. Knowing that his brother was going to do what he could to help lessened the tightening band around his chest when he thought of what was to come.

But the one saving grace was that in this country… money could make miracles happen.

And money was something Hope had plenty of.

HOPE EMERGED FROM the shower feeling slightly better, but no less confused.

She was surprised to see a folded tank top and shorts awaiting her on the bed, but J.T. was nowhere to be found. Hope lifted the shirt and smiled quizzically at the obvious tourist fare, but was grateful for the chance to wear something clean and not ripped to shreds.

The only logical explanation was that J.T. had found the clothes and left them for her to change into.

Okay, admit it… That was very thoughtful.

"Yes," she answered herself with a hint of exasperation. "It was very nice and I certainly don't deserve his thoughtfulness after the way I acted."

Hope supposed she ought to apologize to J.T. for going psycho on him earlier. It wasn't his fault that she was confused by her feelings. It wasn't like her to get all emotional and immature, either. Egad, she despised women like that. If a hidden camera had caught that little display, she surely would've died of mortification.

"Who are you talking to?"

Hope whirled, clutching the towel to her body. "Oh!" she said, laughing nervously. "I didn't hear you come in."

"I figured that when you were having a conversation with no one. Unless you failed to tell me you're the Psychic Scientist, who talks to ghosts."

She cast him a dark look. "Not psychic. And yes, I was talking to myself. I do that sometimes. Helps me to reason things out when I'm otherwise stuck."

"And what did you conclude from your little conversation?"

"Oh, c'mon, you know what I said," she said, her cheeks burning. The smile on his lips was almost contagious. So was the hunger in his eyes. Which reminded her that she was still naked under her towel. She snatched up her clothes and said over her shoulder, "Thanks for the change of clothes!" before disappearing into the bathroom again.

The bathroom was rapidly becoming her safe place.

Stop running away from confrontation! Be an adult. Channel your inner strong, confident woman!

Right.

Hope dressed, took a minute to compose herself and then returned to the bedroom, where she found J.T. waiting—and looking sexy as ever in his newly procured board shorts and bare chest. Shouldn't there be a law against a man looking so sinfully hot?

Get back on point. And stop staring at the dark blond happy trail disappearing behind his waistband! Good grief, it was like an arrow straight to that lovely...

Dragging her gaze away from his groin, she drew a deep breath and decided to rip off the bandage, so to speak, by going straight to the point. "Look, I was inexcusably irrational after our...mutually satisfying sexual encounter and I hope we can get past my behavior and chalk it up to the stress of the last few days. I want to reassure you that I am not, under most circumstances, a shrill, immature woman."

"Good to know."

She nodded. "Yes. I mean, I don't know what came over me." More nervous laughter ensued and she wondered if she sounded like an idiot. Hope wagged her finger at him like a schoolmarm, because, you know, the idiot ship had already sailed. "You are quite talented with your...well, everything. But I'm sure you know that already."

"Thank you?" J.T.'s sensual smile lit up her insides like a Christmas parade. *Oh, dear.* How were they going to sleep side by side without screwing like bunnies until morning?

"Okay, as wonderful and fun as it was...we can't do that again," she told him, affecting a stern position. "I meant what I said about keeping things professional and I think that aside from that momentary lapse in judgment, we should be able to stick to our guns and keep our hands to ourselves."

"Sure."

Why was he readily agreeing with everything she was saying? She eyed him with suspicion. "Are you just saying what I want to hear?"

"Yep."

Frustration rolled through her. "J.T., you're not making this any easier. Don't you agree that continuing to sleep together is a bad idea?"

"If you're a cuddler, then we might have a problem. I sleep hot."

I bet you do, you hot piece of ass!

Her cheeks flared and she was extremely grateful that J.T. was not privy to her private thoughts.

"Are you going to be deliberately difficult? Just agree with me that we shouldn't have sex again and I'll drop it. We can pretend it never happened."

At that J.T. pushed away from the bedpost and came to her, invading her personal space with delicious deliberate abandon, and she found her breath in short supply again.

When he was close enough to sink into those luscious lips, he quirked a cocky grin and said, "Honey, if you can keep your hands to yourself, so can I. But if you keep that pot on high, something's gonna bubble over."

Appropriate metaphor. She wanted to stay strong, to remember all the reasons why it was a bad idea to get cozy with J.T., but that man had superhuman sex powers and it really wasn't fair.

He laughed. "See? You're doing it again."

Hope startled. Good gravy, were her thoughts transparent? She swallowed and lifted her chin. "And what exactly am I doing?"

"Eyeing me like you want to eat me alive."

Oh, damn.

Just the thought of that cock sliding inside her, pounding, demanding, made her shudder delicately with growing need.

"See?" he said softly before kissing her thoroughly. "That's what I'm talking about. You make it hard to be good. Actually…you just make it hard. Period."

"Oh?" And when her hand drifted, of its own accord, to the growing bulge in his shorts, she lost all reason as to why this was a bad idea.

Suddenly, the idea of round two sounded like the best idea ever.

7

HE WAS HEARING what Hope was putting down and a part of him agreed wholeheartedly that tangling with a client was bad business, but the part of him that was in charge was like, *Shut the hell up and get out of my way.*

There was no cycling down at this point. All he could do was hang on for dear life and hope they didn't crash and burn on the way down.

But Hope had nailed it—he was reckless, but right about now, as he was peeling the clothes from her luscious body, he couldn't count that as a weakness.

Her breasts were perfect globes with delicate dusky pink tips that begged to be sucked and teased, and he was happy to oblige.

The hardened nipples pebbled under his tongue as Hope moaned beneath him, wrapping her legs around his torso, capturing him as surely as he'd captured her.

They rolled and she landed on top, casting a saucy grin as she teased his cock with the heat of her slick folds. He wanted to push up into her, impale her with his length, but she prevented him by moving just out of reach.

Her laughter was like sultry music, a beat guaranteed to make him want her forever.

"Not so fast," she purred, sliding down his body to take him into her mouth.

J.T.'s eyes fluttered shut on the pleasure of her warm mouth sucking and teasing, moving up and down the shaft with sensual, deliberate movements that sent him into space. The air in his lungs seized and he saw stars as she tenderly cupped his balls, the warmth of her hand a sweet contrast to the wicked things she was doing to the head of his cock, drilling the hole at the top with that clever tongue.

And just as he was about to burst, she stopped and climbed his body, settling her sweet core right at his greedy mouth, and he was more than happy to kiss those fragrant lips.

He gripped her ass with both hands as she ground herself against his face. His muffled moans filled the room as she gasped, crying out as he toyed with the little pleasure nub as surely as she'd played with him.

J.T. wanted her to shatter beneath his tongue, wanted to lap up her juices as she shuddered and quaked to her completion, but Hope, the little she-devil, had other plans.

Right before she came, she lifted herself off, crying, "Not yet!" and shimmied down to sink down on his cock, taking every inch with a satisfied groan that he echoed.

Was this heaven? Hope riding his cock as though there were no tomorrow?

God, yes.

The view was spectacular, better than any erotic dream he'd ever had.

Hell, better than any late-night porn.

Hope, in the throes of passion, was better than anything he could've imagined.

And it was all he needed to blast off like a rocket.

"Holy f—!" The words were choked off by the intense pleasure rolling through him, crashing like buildings under

demo until there was nothing left of his ability to think but ash and rubble.

Hope found her release and collapsed on top of him, her weight a wonderful pressure on his chest as she rasped deep gasping breaths, his cock still buried in her hot, pulsating core.

With the last bit of strength he had, he gave her one final push, and she shuddered again as her entire body tensed and she came again.

"Good God," she said weakly. "I'll never get enough of that."

She spoke the simple truth for them both.

Even if it was the worst thing to do…even if there was absolutely no future in their hooking up, they both knew that they'd bang each other senseless for as long as it was possible.

After that?

Hell, who knew.

They had to survive the next forty-eight hours first.

HOPE EYED THE rusty older-model truck and then looked back at J.T.

"Are you sure?" she asked in a low voice so as not to offend the driver Juan had managed to find. "It doesn't look…safe."

"Beggars can't be choosers," J.T. reminded her in an equally private tone as he helped her into the back. They settled onto the faded pillows and blankets, and J.T. smiled at Juan. "Let's just get to the airfield and then we'll figure out the next step."

Hope nodded and handed Juan a hefty tip for his services. The boy's face split into a happy grin and he ran off, clutching the money.

"You know that was probably the equivalent of his entire month's wage," J.T. said as the truck lumbered onto the highway. "His family will eat good tonight."

"It's easy to forget how blessed we are when we're locked away in our ivory towers," Hope murmured, thinking of the contents of her pack and how they could level a village like this within days. Innocent lives were at stake. She glanced at J.T., struck by how easily he took everything in stride, even the crappiest situation, and wished she could be like that.

J.T. had procured some sunglasses and was enjoying the wind in his hair. Of course, he looked incredibly sexy, instantly reminding her of what they'd done to each other all night.

How was it that this man—her complete opposite—had the power to take her breath away?

She clutched her pack a little more tightly, wondering what J.T. would think of her if he knew what exactly she was transporting.

Would he hate her?

If she weren't such a coward, she'd just tell him and let the chips fall where they may, but there was no way in hell she was going to do that.

Not only because it was a huge security risk, but because she feared his reaction.

It was stupid, but she couldn't bear the thought of J.T. looking at her with disgust.

Would it matter that she'd never anticipated that her research would be perverted from its original purpose in this way?

Of course not. There was a part of her that'd worried about the potential implications if it fell into the wrong hands, but she'd been too excited about the breakthroughs to listen to that niggling voice of doubt.

Now she wished she'd scrapped the project.

Maybe her boss would still be alive.

A tear threatened to escape and she turned her face away from J.T. so he wouldn't see her cry.

So many things she'd do differently.

But none of it mattered if she couldn't get the package to the facility.

That was what she needed to focus on.

The rest… Well, the rest was just noise.

J.T. MUST'VE DOZED, not surprising since he hadn't gotten much sleep last night, but when he woke up, they were heading into a dirty, cramped part of the city that looked stuck in the past.

Dogs ran in the streets along with scraggly children wearing rags, and it was hard not to see the abject poverty everywhere.

It was a different world than most Americans were accustomed to, but his time in the military had exposed him to cultures vastly different from their own.

However, Hope was a different story.

He could see the worry in her expression as she saw children of all ages on the streets when they should've been in school. He didn't have to tell her that most of the street kids would never see the inside of a classroom and the cycle of poverty would continue.

The truck rumbled to a stop outside a grimy strip mall that didn't look safe at all, but their ride was over.

"The airport is that way," the driver said in a thick accent, pointing west. He waited pointedly, eyeing Hope's pack, and she hastily gave him some cash.

"Thank you," she murmured, shooting an uncertain look at J.T. as the driver took off. "Please tell me we didn't just ride four hours in the back of a truck to be murdered outside this building."

"We need to find a place where I can buy a phone," he said, trying to keep her focused. They stuck out like a sore thumb, practically wearing signs on their backs that said "Rob Me", and he wasn't about to take any chances.

Although his first thought was that the driver had screwed them, he quickly realized that he'd actually done them a favor. "Look, there's an electronics store. They ought to have a phone I can buy. My brother is working on getting us a plane, but I need to be able to contact him."

"When did you call your brother?"

"When we first got into Lacanjá."

"Did you tell him anything about me?" Her voice held an anxious edge and he sensed it had everything to do with that pack and not with their hooking up. He would've preferred her anxiety be due to the hooking up for some reason.

"No, I didn't say anything. Just that you were a client and we ran into some trouble."

"Good. Please keep it that way," she said, visibly relieved. "Let's go find you a phone."

He wanted to say something about her relief, but he kept his mouth shut. They had bigger fish to fry.

They walked into the small store, and as luck would have it, there was a wall of pay-as-you-go phones with international calling capabilities. Hope threw down her American Express card and they were good to go.

"Is there a limit to that thing?" he asked, curious. Hope didn't answer, just gave him a short smile. "All right, I get it. Anything associated with your work, your employer, that damn pack on your back is off-limits."

"It's just better that way."

"Better for who?"

"For us both."

Somehow he doubted that, but now was not the time to pick at that particular issue.

"You call your brother and I'll go get some more cash,"

she said, cinching up her pack, then pointing to the small bank across the street.

"I'll go with you," he said, uncomfortable with the idea of Hope traipsing around with wads of cash in this neighborhood.

"It's just across the street. I'll be fine."

"Look around, Hope. This isn't exactly Middle America. Don't be dumb. Dumb pretty ladies get snatched off the street and sold into slavery and it's not a *Pretty Woman* type story."

Hope paled and quickly nodded. "Okay, maybe you're right. Except about the dumb part."

"You're right—you're not dumb," he corrected himself. "But you're damn stubborn and in the wrong situations that can be just as dangerous."

"You've made your point," Hope said, glowering. "Can we just go get some cash?"

He pocketed the phone and they hustled across the street to the small bank. Within a relatively short time, Hope had managed to procure a sizable amount of cash, which she promptly stuffed in her pack, out of sight, but J.T. was a bit leery of having all the cash in one spot. All it would take was an industrious thief to swipe her pack and all of their resources would disappear.

Still, he knew it was pointless to try to convince her otherwise, particularly when she was so paranoid about that damn pack, so he didn't waste his breath.

Outside the bank, J.T. called Teagan.

"J.T.?" Teagan answered. When J.T. confirmed it was him, Teagan's relief was evident in his tone. "Man, I was starting to sweat."

"We lucked out and managed to find a store where I could buy a phone. I called you as soon as I could. Did you find us a plane?"

"Yeah, it took some string pulling, but I found a plane

you can charter. It'll cost you, but you said your client has enough green?"

"Yeah," J.T. answered. "She says her company will pay whatever it takes to get her to the facility."

"Have you found out exactly what you're transporting?" The worry in Teagan's voice mirrored J.T.'s own growing anxiety about Hope's package. "I mean, you know something feels off about this. Why the hell were you getting shot at?"

He couldn't answer his brother, because he still didn't know. And he certainly couldn't go into detail about the situation with Hope standing right there listening to his every word.

"Who's my contact?" J.T. asked, changing the subject.

Teagan took the hint. "Your contact is Alejandro Ruiz. You'll find him at a private hangar at Comitán. He's agreed to take you to South America."

"Good work. Thanks, bro. I owe you one."

"Don't worry about that. Just come home alive. I've got a bad feeling about this."

"You and me both," he agreed in a low tone. "I'll be in touch."

He hung up and pocketed the phone. "We're good to go. Our contact is Alejandro Ruiz and he's waiting for us at Comitán."

Relief spread across Hope's features. "Thank God." Impulsively, she lifted on her toes and brushed a kiss across J.T.'s lips. The sudden action startled them both and she immediately started apologizing. "I'm so sorry. That was inappropriate. I was just so happy…"

He knew the smart thing was to agree with her, but he liked kissing her and he liked that her first impulse was to kiss him.

J.T. ignored the voice of reason in his head and reached for her. "If you're going to do it, might as well make it worth your while, right?" And then he sealed his mouth to hers, drinking in the feel of her soft lips pressed against his, the taste of her tongue in his mouth. When he finally released her, she looked thoroughly well kissed, and it was a good look on her. Sexy as hell. But then, Hope didn't need any help in that department. He grasped her hand, saying, "Let's go. Time's wasting," before she regained her sense and started blathering on about rules and appropriate behavior.

Because, honestly, he didn't want to hear it.

She didn't want to be honest about what was in that damn pack and he didn't want to stop kissing her.

They both had problems.

8

ALEJANDRO RUIZ WAS a short, stout man with a ready smile and a twinkle in his brown eyes that immediately put Hope at ease after their bumpy ride to Comitán.

Hope paid him an exorbitant sum without blinking, just happy they were on their way. The faster they were up in the air, the faster they got to South America, where she could destroy this ticking time bomb on her back.

J.T. helped Hope climb into the small plane and then, after they were buckled in, Alejandro started his preflight checklist. Both Hope and J.T. slipped on headsets to protect their ears from the sound of the engines as well as to communicate.

"So where is this research facility located?" J.T. asked once they were airborne.

Hope hesitated to answer. Originally, she'd planned to turn J.T. loose as soon as they landed in São Paulo, Brazil, trusting that she could find transport to the remote location on her own. But since the situation had changed drastically, she wasn't sure heading off on her own was such a smart idea.

"It's a remote area in Brazil, not very populated."

"Makes sense for a supersecret privatized pharmaceutical facility," J.T. remarked with his signature dry humor. "So, what's going to happen when we get to this undisclosed location?"

This was the part that had her awake at night. The fact was, no one knew she was going to the facility to destroy the samples. She'd been ordered to report to the South American lab to protect the samples, but when her supervisor, Tanya, intercepted a message that someone within Tessara was brokering a deal for the dangerous bioweapon, she'd sent Hope off under the guise of bringing the samples for protection.

The plan had been for Tanya to accompany her, but then Tanya had been gunned down in broad daylight outside a sandwich shop, changing everything.

She was doing J.T. a disservice by keeping him in the dark, but she couldn't think of any other way to accomplish what she'd set out to do without putting him in even more danger.

"You seem on edge," he said. "Are you okay?"

"I'm good." Hope faked what she hoped appeared to be a bright smile. "Just relieved to be back on schedule."

J.T. settled against the worn leather chair with a nod, but there was something behind his eyes that told her he wasn't buying her act.

If only she could tell him. She'd known J.T. for only a few days, but she trusted him more than she trusted anyone else in her life.

Maybe it was that extreme-situation-hormonal-chemical thing striking again, because she just wanted to lean into him, tell him everything and ask him for advice on what to do next.

Even if her situation hadn't required her silence, her stubborn refusal to play the damsel in distress would've kept her from sharing, too.

Sometimes being a strong, independent woman had its drawbacks.

Exhausted, both mentally and physically, Hope drifted off to sleep, happy to forget at least for a little while that her life would never be the same after they landed in São Paulo.

J.T. WAS GLAD for the sleep he'd snagged in the back of the truck because he wouldn't have been able to sleep on the plane with a pilot he didn't know. It wasn't that he didn't trust Teagan's connections; it was that he didn't trust anyone in the cockpit besides himself or his brother.

In other words, it wasn't personal.

Hope was fast asleep. He felt vaguely bad for keeping her up all night, but then, he couldn't exactly feel too bad, because he'd do it again in a heartbeat.

That woman was hotter than any woman he'd ever been with. The smart-and-sexy-scientist gig was working for him, better than what he'd thought was his thing.

But now that he'd been with Hope, he found his usual taste distasteful.

He used to like a woman who wasn't too smart.

He didn't want to discuss politics or global warming when he was stripping down. He wanted a woman who liked it dirty and hot and didn't waste time trying to have an intellectual connection.

Now?

Hope had ruined him.

J.T. found her smarts incredibly sexy. He liked the idea of seducing her mind *and* body.

Tall order for a woman as intelligent and highly educated as Hope.

And the challenge fired him up in a way that'd been missing for quite some time in his life.

So what did that mean? After this gig, assuming they

made it out alive, they were destined to go their separate ways.

Hope hadn't once suggested that after this was all over they would continue to see each other.

Well, he hadn't, either. But he hadn't received any green light on her end that she'd be open to that suggestion, so he wasn't about to put himself out there only to be shot down.

Yeah, not so crazy about the idea of being rejected.

But he was equally bothered by the idea of walking away, never to see each other again.

Hell, he was turning into a woman.

He knew a little about Brazil and figured they were going to land in São Paulo, but as they flew over the main city, J.T. got a bad feeling in his gut.

"Where are we landing? We just passed São Paulo."

"I don't have clearance for São Paulo. I have a friend with a small airfield, off the grid. We will land there. No worries, friend. I will take care of you and your lady."

Yeah, J.T. didn't like the sound of that. But what could he do? They had no choice, but to ride it out and hope that Alejandro wasn't about to murder them.

All for that damn pack. He wished he were a different sort of person and could rifle through the pack without her knowledge without suffering a bout of conscience.

He wanted to tell himself that it wasn't the fact that she had secrets. Hell, they all had secrets, right? There were things in his past he didn't want people poking around in, but his secrets weren't shooting at them. Or was he just being a whiny baby, pissed because she was keeping some things close to the vest?

He wasn't accustomed to women holding themselves apart. Usually, women were pushing for a deeper connection, when he was the one trying to get away.

He liked to tell himself that he was a confirmed bachelor—a happily confirmed bachelor—but the fact was, it was easier to remain without strings than to trust another human being with something as battered and bruised as his heart.

He wondered what Hope would think of his past if she knew everything he'd been through while serving in the military. He wasn't one of those people who lamented the loss of his innocence when called to serve his country, but there were some things in his past that he would love to forget.

J.T. knew basically nothing about Hope aside from what she had told him. Hell, she could be lying through her teeth and he wouldn't be the wiser.

Hope was rapidly becoming like a drug in his system. He wanted more even though he knew more would likely kill him. Everything about her set him on fire.

Even her secrets.

It had been a long time since he'd had to use his military training, but it came back like riding a bike—the threat of a sketchy situation had him on alert. He didn't like the idea of landing in some airfield in the middle of nowhere. The fact that somebody was trying to kill them didn't make him feel very safe, despite Alejandro smiling and nodding as if everything was kosher.

"So where is this airfield?"

"No worries, friend. I've done this before. You are in good hands."

Yeah, that didn't fill him with relief. South America was nearly as bad as Mexico with illegal drug running. They might have just gone from the frying pan to the fire. J.T. thought of the wad of cash Hope was carrying and he couldn't have felt more like a Christmas hog than if he'd been bound and trussed up with an apple in his mouth.

He would've felt more assured if he'd been able to talk to Teagan's contact first.

Hope stirred and yawned as she awoke. She blinked

blearily at J.T. with a sleepy smile and he returned a brief smile so as not to worry her.

"Are we there yet?"

"We're not landing in São Paulo," he told her. She reacted with a flutter of alarm, but he quickly tried to reassure her, if only to keep her calm. "Alejandro doesn't have clearance for the city's airfield, but he has a friend with a private airstrip. We're landing there."

"Private airstrip?" she repeated, echoing his own trepidation. "No, that's not going to work. We need transportation. How are we going to get to the facility without someone to take us?"

Alejandro was listening and interjected, "No worries, senorita. We have it all worked out. My friend will meet us and he will take you to your destination."

Hope settled against her seat, but retained an air of worry. She sent him a look that asked, *Are we in trouble?* and he couldn't rightly allay her fears when he shared them.

But he couldn't do anything about the situation from where he sat. They'd just have to ride it out and remain on their toes.

Maybe he was overreacting.

Maybe Alejandro was truly a good guy, and when this was all over, they'd laugh and laugh about their suspicions.

But maybe the joke was on them and they were being delivered to the very people they were trying to avoid.

His gut told him they were screwed.

9

Hope wanted to believe J.T., but she sensed he was lying for her benefit. The deal had been transport to São Paulo, not some unidentified airstrip in the middle of the Amazon rain forest.

This felt as messed up as the police report that said Tanya had been killed in a random robbery gone wrong.

Her mouth dried of spit and she wanted to cry. So much for being a strong, independent woman.

J.T. reached over and squeezed her hand, and she gratefully squeezed back, needing that human touch.

If J.T. had a plan, he certainly couldn't share, given that Alejandro could hear their every word. Every muscle was tensed and her stomach threatened to rebel.

It'd been only a week, but she hardly remembered her old life of being blissfully unaware of the intrigue and danger that was just around the corner.

Had it been only three weeks ago that she and Tanya had shared a frozen pizza in the lab cafeteria, too excited about their breakthrough to spend more than fifteen minutes wolfing down some carbs so they could power through to the next step?

Her life had consisted of work and science for so long she couldn't remember much else.

And she'd loved it.

A social life had been secondary to the important work they'd been doing.

Tanya had shared her enthusiasm, her thirst for discovery. Neither had questioned whether they should've kept going.

And now Tanya was dead.

Her family grieving.

And Hope was flying in a bucket of bolts to some uncharted airfield in the middle of South America with no idea whether or not they were heading into a neatly laid trap or finally heading into a safe zone.

Well, if the sick tremble in her stomach was any indication, they were not arrowing toward safety.

She pulled off her headset, needing space from everything.

Even J.T.

He seemed to understand and didn't press her. Under normal circumstances, a man like J.T. would've been fun to get to know, but then, under normal circumstances, she and J.T. never would've circulated in the same circles, so they never would've met.

Memories of their intimate times flashed in her mind and her cheeks warmed considerably even as she savored them for the tiny reprieve the remembered pleasure provided.

Good Lord, that man could make a woman forget her own name.

A quick covert glance at J.T. confirmed that he was ridiculously handsome. Having sex with him had only intensified the sexy quotient by half. She wasn't the kind of woman to lose her head over a guy.

But then, J.T. wasn't like most guys, either.

She shouldn't have been ruminating about sexy times with her hot pilot when they were potentially flying to their doom, but maybe that was the best time to think of better things.

If they were about to die, she was happy she'd slept with J.T.

In fact, if they hadn't had sex and she was suddenly staring down the business end of a gun, she would've been really pissed that she hadn't taken advantage of her opportunity before dying.

Sheesh, Hope, way to stay positive.

But she was too frazzled to cling to false hope. Her sixth sense was shrieking right now and it was that gut instinct that'd kept her alive when she'd managed to walk into J.T.'s life, so it didn't do her any favors to ignore that little voice now.

And something told her that J.T. was listening to the same warning bells.

The question was…what the hell were they going to do about it?

ALEJANDRO LANDED ON the dirt airfield with minimal fuss, never losing his happy smile even as they climbed out of the small plane to find a black car waiting. When four muscled thugs erupted from the vehicle, J.T. wasn't surprised, though he'd been hoping that his hunch was wrong.

Hope turned to Alejandro with a stiff upper lip, demanding to know what was going on, though her voice bordered on shrill in her panic.

"I paid you for safe transport. What is the meaning of this?"

"And I have put you safely on South American soil. I have fulfilled my end of the bargain, senorita. As you can imagine, times are hard and my family has needs. I cannot afford to give up opportunity." Alejandro smiled as if his conscience was clear and then mock-saluted the thugs, saying, "I have done as requested."

One of the thugs pulled a bundle of cash and tossed it at Alejandro, and he caught it handily with a bigger grin. "Adios!" he called out as he returned to his plane, leaving them to their fates.

One of the thugs, squeezed into an ill-fitting suit, removed his sunglasses and tucked them into an interior pocket. "Someone is very interested in meeting you, Miss Larsen."

J.T. caught the flash of a revolver butt, and he knew their chances of getting away without taking a bullet to the back were slim to none. Not to mention they were deep in the Amazon jungle, where there were hundreds of ways to die a grisly and painful death that might make a bullet seem like a mercy.

"And who might that be?" J.T. asked, stalling for time while he tried to think of a plan.

But they weren't in a talking mood.

A curt nod from the one in charge, and another thug grabbed Hope and the other two mobbed J.T., landing a few good punches to his gut and jaw before he could defend himself. A momentary blackout gave them enough time to tie his feet and hands and toss him into the trunk.

He heard Hope scream as they forced her into the backseat, but a quick slap cut the sound short. Rage cleared away the cobwebs of his muzzy head and he closed his eyes, calming himself before he did something stupid.

He needed to be smart. They were transporting them someplace, likely to the person who'd been shooting at them back in California and had been searching for them ever since.

Logic said they wouldn't hurt Hope, because they needed her—or more specifically, they needed what was in her damn pack. But that didn't leave any protection promise for himself. Chances were they were going to toss him out as a loose end as soon as they reached their destination, which meant he had to find a way out of this trunk before then.

He caught muffled laughter between the thugs, but nothing from Hope. Perhaps the force of the slap had knocked her out. J.T. wanted to kill whoever had touched Hope, but he willed his rage to cool so he could think rationally.

J.T. wiggled his fingers and found enough slack to work his wrists until he managed to free one hand, then the other. But because there wasn't much room in the trunk, getting his feet free was more difficult.

Sweat poured down his face as he concentrated on the task and not on the confines of the tight space.

Back in the Air Force he'd taken small-space training, learning how to manipulate his body and regulate his breathing to avoid panic. He'd never had to use the training during his military career, but it was coming in handy right now.

"Thank you, Sergeant Thack, you cranky bastard," he muttered as he finally freed his feet. Thack had put J.T. in the training as a punishment for messing around with his oldest daughter. Those six weeks had been a bitch—the worst time of his life.

Until this moment, of course.

J.T. fished his phone from his pocket, which thankfully the thugs hadn't bothered to check, and quickly called Teagan. The service was sketchy and the connection weak, but the call finally went through.

"Teagan," J.T. whispered when his brother answered. "Trouble."

Not messing around, Teagan went on alert. "What's wrong? What's that noise?"

"That would be the sound of the road from the inside

of a trunk, in case you've ever wondered what that's like. It sucks. Don't try it."

"You're in a trunk?"

"Yeah, with the presumption that this is far safer than what's going to happen once we reach our destination. Our pilot sold us out."

"Son of a bitch," Teagan swore. "That miserable cuss. I'm going to feed him his balls."

"Never mind that. Help me think of a way out of this mess."

"Okay, okay, let me think… Is it a newer car?"

"From what I remember…yeah."

"Okay, the tire iron will be in a side compartment that you should be able to open. That's your best chance at a weapon. When they open that trunk door, you catch them by surprise and start swinging. They won't expect it and it might give you a few minutes to run."

"That's not much of a plan for Hope."

"You can't help your client if you're dead."

Couldn't argue with that.

"I'll track your position through the phone's GPS and call in a few favors."

"The last favor you called in landed me in a trunk," he reminded Teagan ruefully. "I'm not sure I trust your favors."

"You got better options?"

"Nope."

"Then shut up and let me do what I can."

"Hurry, man—it's not in my destiny to die in the Amazon jungle. I have it on good authority I'm supposed to die in the arms of a buxom blonde with a smile on my face."

"Just do your best to lose yourself in that jungle. I will find you."

"Yes, sir," J.T. said, trying to keep it light for his

brother's sake. The situation was shit. The chances of survival were slim. And they both knew it.

Jokes were just J.T.'s way of dealing with the bad odds and Teagan knew it.

J.T. forced a smile as he said, "Hey, I have an idea... Let's sell Blue Yonder and buy a boat. We can charge hot tourists in bikinis to charter them around the Caribbean or something."

Teagan replied with a hint of unexpected humor, "Neither one of us knows anything about boats. We're flyboys, remember?"

J.T. grinned in spite of the situation. "Yeah, I remember. So get me a damn plane. I've had enough of this place to last a lifetime."

"I'm on it, brother. Stay alive."

The line went dead and J.T. closed his eyes briefly, wondering if that was the last time he would speak to Teagan. This was one scrape that Teagan might not be able to patch up.

And he felt like crap that the burden fell to his brother. Again.

He'd like to live long enough to save his brother's ass for a change one of these days.

Put that on the agenda for later.

For now...time to save your own ass.

10

HOPE'S JAW ACHED like a mother, but she kept her complaints to herself. She certainly didn't want another slap from that beefy thug's hand. The last one had nearly taken her head off.

She worried about J.T., thrown in the trunk like a sack of potatoes. Did he have enough air? Had they killed him? Icy fear drenched her thoughts as her anxiety rose. He couldn't be dead. J.T. would figure out a way to…escape a moving vehicle with tied hands and feet?

Yeah, he wasn't a magician.

The car rolled up to a massive, intricately designed wrought iron gate buried deep within the jungle. The driver punched in a code and the gates slowly opened.

Wherever they were going, it was heavily fortified. Armed guards—more than likely hired mercenaries—walked the perimeter of the fencing with hard eyes, incapable of mercy.

They rolled up to a palatial mansion with a fringe of white banisters along the tiered balconies that screamed of opulence and dirty money. Who built a fortress in the jungle unless they didn't want to be found?

Hope shuddered and swallowed, more frightened of

this place than she'd been of sleeping out in the open of the Mexican jungle.

Thinking fast, she banked on the assumption that whoever had commanded her presence had to know what she was carrying, so she was needed alive. But likely J.T. was baggage they didn't need, which meant as soon as they opened that trunk, the clock was ticking on his life.

She couldn't bear to let anything happen to him when it was her fault that he was in this mess. Time for a show of audacious boldness.

"If anything happens to me or my friend, your employer won't get what he's after."

"Shut up. You'll do exactly as you're told."

Hope blinked back the surge of fear as her throat threatened to close and held her course with forced bravery. "What I have in my possession could kill each of you within hours. I would enjoy watching your skin boil as your insides melt and your bones disintegrate. The interesting thing is that it doesn't exactly kill you right away, but you're quite aware of all the damage that's happening to your body. In a way…it's sort of what I imagine it would feel like to be eaten alive."

That got their attention.

The two men flanking her on either side shifted nervously to give her more room. She smiled.

"She's just trying to freak you out," the driver warned as he rolled to a stop in front of the mansion.

"It's working," the thug in the passenger seat grumbled, unsure of the situation. "What if she ain't lying?"

"Indeed," Hope agreed with a chilly smile, then embellished a little for flair. "That's what I do for a living— I create new and interesting ways to kill a human being without leaving a trace."

Okay, so she'd embellished a lot. But they didn't know that and her very survival depended on selling that lie,

so she was going to own it as if she were more dangerous than them.

The thugs bailed from the car a little more quickly than
before and she smothered a shaky laugh. Well, at least that
part of her plan was working.

The thugs looked to the driver for direction. "What do
you want us to do with him?"

The driver paused, plainly unsure if Hope was bluffing and weighing whether or not he should risk it. Finally,
he grumbled, "Bring him. Boss can figure out what to do
with him."

Hope breathed a secret sigh of relief, but as the thugs
opened the trunk to retrieve J.T., a sudden flurry of motion, blood spattering and cursing ensued as J.T. sprang
from the trunk like an avenging demon, swinging a tire
iron with the intent of cracking skulls.

The driver shoved her to the ground and charged J.T.,
deflecting a swing of the tire iron with his forearm and
landing a punch to J.T.'s jaw.

J.T. recovered and swung out with his left foot, con-
necting with the man's kneecap, driving him straight to
the ground.

It was like watching gladiators pummel each other in
the ring. Hope could only gape as they grappled, tossing
each other around, landing punches and knocking each
other sideways until J.T. cracked a good hit across the
thug's face, sending him straight to the dirt.

Elated by his bloody victory, she scrambled to her feet
to run with him, but he stopped her with a terse, "You
stay," which instantly baffled and hurt her.

"What are you talking about? You can't leave me here!"

Bleeding from the nose and lip, J.T. shocked her when
he shouted, "I'll be back! Trust me!" and bolted for the
perimeter like a felon evading the guards.

For a long moment, Hope continued to stare with incredulous shock in the direction J.T. had disappeared, unable to comprehend what he'd just done.

He'd left her!

That rotten son of a bitch! Here she was worrying about *his* safety and he went and bailed on her like a coward?

"I hope you get eaten by an anaconda!" she called out, her indignation blotting out the fear of being left on her own with the scary thugs and only God knew what else.

The driver rose, limping from his abused knee, and then, after his fellow thugs had risen slowly, holding their heads and bitching about their injuries, he barked orders. "Find that bastard and bring him back to me!"

They cast dirty looks, but did as they were told, leaving the driver and Hope alone.

"Your friend is going to die for that," he promised Hope with a glower, then jerked his head and growled, "Start walking."

He pushed her and she stumbled, refusing to let him see her tremble. She was smarter than this Neanderthal. Lifting her chin, she threw him an icy glare that she hoped promised a grisly, torturous death and walked into the cool confines of the huge main house.

Ceiling fans pushed around the humid air, while native flora hung from huge pots, lending a wild look to the cultured and opulent surroundings. She wouldn't have been surprised to see a monkey pop out from behind a huge potted fern or a snake wind itself free from one of the vines and loop itself around the banisters.

The man pushed her into a large office, the walls decorated with animal trophies that immediately made her queasy, barked, "Wait here," and then he left.

The room was richly appointed with a definite masculine touch—above and beyond the dead animal heads, of course—so when a sharply dressed man with hair that was lightly graying at the temples walked in with a glittering smile that made her want to hide, she knew she was looking at the man who had likely killed Tanya.

Maybe he hadn't pulled the trigger, but he'd surely given the order.

Actually, she thought with another glance at the animal trophies, maybe he had pulled the trigger. Maybe he was one of those sick freaks who enjoyed hunting human beings for sport.

She couldn't help the shudder, which he caught, prompting him to smile.

"Would you care for a cool beverage?" he asked solicitously, as if her arrival hadn't been under duress and practically a hostage situation, his voice colored with a rich Spanish accent. "The locals make a delicious tropical drink called *ulubomba* that's made from the crushed *cupuaçu*, a creamy fruit that tastes of chocolate, banana, pear, passion fruit and pineapple. I confess, it's been a bit of an obsession for me since the first time I tasted it."

Hope stared as he levered himself into an expansive leather executive chair behind a huge mahogany desk. "Are you kidding me right now?" she asked, going straight to the point. "Why have you kidnapped me and brought me here against my will?"

"Ah…" He steepled his fingers and said, "My apologies for the rough transport, but you are a difficult person to procure."

"Perhaps a phone call would've been more efficient," she returned, narrowing her gaze. "Forgive me for being less than eager to make your acquaintance after you killed my friend and tried to shoot me out of the sky."

She was going off a hunch, but he didn't try to deny it. Spreading his fingers as if caught with his hand in the cookie jar, he said, "One must regrettably crack a few eggs to make an omelet. As a scientist, I'm sure you can appreciate that concept."

"My friend was no egg for your omelet. She was a human being with family and friends who are grieving her loss."

"If it appeases your ruffled feathers, it was not my intention to have your plane shot down. That was an error in judgment on my employee's behalf. Thankfully, we discovered you are quite resourceful. I was impressed with your ability to evade my attempts to bring you here."

"Am I supposed to be flattered? Who the hell are you?"

"Let's not waste energy bickering about things in the past, as the future is what interests me most. My name is Anso DeLeon. It is my pleasure to finally meet the woman who will help me make history."

"You're insane. I wouldn't help you walk across the street after what you've done."

He rose and walked to a lion's head hung midsnarl on the wall. Gesturing to the trophy, he said, "You see this here? This is an African lion, the alpha. He had testicles the size of dinner plates and lionesses twitching their tails in his face all day long. It was a genuine pleasure to watch him in action, awe inspiring, really. He was living large, king of his universe without apology. I respected that."

"So you responded by killing him and sticking his head on your wall? The cost of your admiration is too high for my blood. Maybe you could've just snapped a picture on your phone like most normal people."

"A picture has no soul," Anso responded as if that made perfect sense. "The local people believe that when they take the life of an animal, they absorb the spirit, the strength of the animal." He stroked the big cat's lifeless cheek. "I ate his heart from his still-warm body. I felt the spirit of this creature become part of me and it was beautiful."

"I think the lion would disagree."

He shrugged. "You will never understand the power of

taking a life," he said, adding, "You are a woman. Your power is to give life. I do not fault you for your ignorance."

Ignorant? Who was Psycho Suave calling ignorant? She held her tongue, choosing bored silence over obvious indignation as her weapon of choice.

Anso mistook her silence for one of acquiescence and smiled indulgently. "You have journeyed far and I have not shown my best hospitality. Let me amend that error. Fresh clothes, a bath and a room fit for a queen await. You will join me for dinner."

She wanted to shout, *Dream on!* but she needed time to think, to process, and she couldn't do that while suffering this bastard's banter. Hope lifted her chin. "Very well," she said stiffly as she bent to pick up her pack, but he stopped her with a cold smile.

"The pack, if you please, will remain with me."

Hope felt the color drain from her cheeks. "My pack stays with me."

Anso smiled and snapped his fingers. Two men appeared. One grabbed her arm while the other scooped the pack up.

"I await your delightful presence at supper."

And then she was dragged away, her pack in the hands of a man whose cultured smile and cold eyes gave her the chills as surely as staring down the business end of a gun aimed at her head.

J.T. RAN UNTIL he was certain he wasn't being followed, and then he collapsed, his chest heaving as he caught his breath under cover of the thick jungle foliage.

Once again, he was lost in the jungle.

And he'd left Hope behind.

It'd been the only way—a calculated risk to protect her safety in the only way he knew how—but it still stung like a bitch to know that she thought he'd abandoned her.

It didn't matter that he'd promised to come for her; she'd watched in disbelief as he'd run away, which probably made him look like a coward.

He cringed.

But how much worse would it have been if Hope had been shot in the back as they both ran?

You can't save her if you're both dead.

Reason was a paltry balm for his shrieking conscience.

J.T. pulled his phone and called his brother, but the call went to voice mail, which meant Teagan was probably already in the air.

Which also meant he had to sit tight, stay alive and wait for his brother to find him so they could go in, rescue Hope and put this wretched place in the rearview mirror.

Staying on the ground was a risky venture—due to both roaming predators and poisonous things that bit—so J.T. took to a tree, climbing the massive thing until he found a branch that he could fashion a small bower from to spend the night. Lashing vines together with broad leaves, he tied himself to the tree and settled in for a long night.

Closing his eyes, he kept his mind purposefully blank. It was too easy to second-guess every decision when he was getting an instant replay every ten seconds, and he couldn't waste energy looking backward.

The jungle cacophony became white noise and J.T. dozed here and there. Why his thoughts drifted to his last tour of duty, he had no idea, but soon he was reliving one of his worst moments.

"Renegade, you are clear to engage."

The static voice of Mission Control crackled in his headset above his mask and J.T.'s gloved hand hovered over the button that would release the heat-seeking missile.

"This is Renegade. Target acquired," he confirmed as his jet split the sky like a hot knife through butter. The mission was a simple one, but highly classified. Deep in the Afghan desert, the hideout of a high-ranking al-Qaeda leader had been supposedly discovered. J.T.'s squadron, the Hell Cats, were charged with carrying out a sensitive mission—take out the leader's lair with minimal civilian casualties.

J.T. didn't hesitate. He pushed the button. "Fox Two is a go. I repeat, Fox Two is a go."

A deadly sidewinder arrowed straight to its intended target and everything went boom.

Except…the intel had been bad.

And J.T. had blown up a small village, killing everyone in the dead of night.

The ensuing investigation had cleared J.T. of any wrong-doing, but that hadn't absolved his conscience. J.T. finished up his tour and hung up his dog tags for good.

Collateral damage, they'd said.

His buddies couldn't understand why J.T. was so shaken up by the mistake.

"Shit happens," Rocco "Rooster" Gianni had said with a shrug. "There had to be some reason that the intel put us there. Maybe they weren't so innocent after all. Let it go, man. You know what they say—war is hell, right?"

"They were innocent people," J.T. said, feeling sick to his stomach. "I didn't sign up to kill women and children."

"I'm telling you, they couldn't have been all that inno-cent. For all we know, they were harboring that SOB and if that's the case, they got what they deserved."

In the end, J.T. just couldn't get right with it and had to end his military career earlier than he'd planned.

Hell, he'd always thought that they'd have to pull his cold, dead fingers from the throttle to get him to stop fly-ing. The thrill of zero-G had always been a bit of an ad-diction.

But fate was a bitch that way.

Guess she'd had different plans for the Carmichael boys.

Why was he thinking of that night? He'd long since put that incident in a locked box and tucked it away.

Maybe because he'd been holding on to Blue Yonder for selfish reasons and should've listened to Teagan from the start when things had begun to sour for their small charter business.

And now he was lashed to a tree in the Amazon jungle with a fairly high probability that he was going to die within the next twenty-four hours and his brother, Teagan, was caught in his mess, too.

Why couldn't he have been gifted with a smidgen of Teagan's levelheaded foresight? No, he was always the one doing something reckless and stupid.

Like taking on a client that his gut plainly told him to steer clear of—and then sleeping with said client.

He supposed he deserved the lecture that was coming.

If he survived.

11

HOPE GAPED AT the filmy gown that she was supposed to wear to dinner and wondered if this was some kind of joke.

It was practically see-through.

And looked like something from the 1940s.

Did this madman think she was going to become part of his jungle harem?

Two alluring Brazilian women wearing next to nothing on their curvaceous bodies entered the room and frowned when they saw that she had not dressed yet.

"Master DeLeon will not be pleased to see you are not appreciative of his gift," the older woman said with pursed lips. "Come, we must dress you quickly. He does not like to be kept waiting."

"He can wait until the parrots start singing 'The Lion Sleeps Tonight' because I'm not wearing that," Hope said, shaking her head emphatically. "It's nearly see-through, and besides, I'd rather *not* dine with *Mr.* DeLeon." There was no way in hell she was calling him *master*. "I'll have my supper in my room, thank you."

The woman narrowed her gaze and shared a look with the younger one. "You are supposed to be very smart, but you seem very stupid to me. You will allow us to help you or Master DeLeon will have someone else come help you, and I doubt they will be as gentle as myself and Ana-Maria."

Hope opened her mouth to protest, but thought better of it. She shuddered at the thought of being "helped" into her dress by DeLeon's thugs. She lifted her chin and said, "Fine, you can help me into that ridiculous dress, but I want to go on record as saying that I think this is absolutely archaic. Women are not property or toys to be dressed up at someone's will. I have a PhD, for crying out loud. I'm not a Barbie doll."

"Your credentials mean nothing here. You are far from America and your American ways. Here, Master DeLeon is king and it would be better for you to recognize this fact before your pretty white skin is whipped from your bones."

Hope tried not to show her fear at the idea of being whipped, but she surely felt the blood drain from her cheeks. She dropped her gaze to the hateful bit of sparkly cloth and gulped down the lump lodged in her throat to stiffly ask, "Will you kindly help me into this dress?"

"Perhaps you do learn quickly." AnaMaria giggled and they flowed around Hope, making quick work of slipping the dress over her shoulders and tugging it over her hips.

Good gravy! The dress clung to every curve, even accentuating the V of her thighs, leaving nothing to the imagination.

AnaMaria worked a bit of magic on Hope's hair, twisting it into an elegant knot on top of her head, leaving a few tendrils to tease her jaw, and the other woman applied makeup with an artistic, though heavy, hand.

"When you are clean and dressed, you are not ugly," AnaMaria said as if surprised. "Pale as milk, but not ugly."

"Gee, thanks," Hope said with a faint glower, still shocked over how the dress clung like a second skin. For a woman who spent most of her life in a lab coat and comfy slacks, this was as far from her usual garb as it could be.

AnaMaria, feeling generous, paused before leaving, saying, "Give Master DeLeon what he wants and you will be treated like a queen. He can be quite a generous lover."

Lover! Oh, hell no. Had she dropped into the twilight zone or a different dimension where women were traded for goods and services? Oh, wait, no, she was just walking a tightwire of danger and intrigue over something she'd invented that could destroy the world!

But there was no use in trying to disabuse the two women of their assumptions, because clearly, it didn't matter. They thought she was an idiot for not encouraging Anso's advances.

From their vantage point, they were pampered princesses and Anso was the king, doling out diamonds and privilege in exchange for their bodies and dignity.

Well, that wasn't going to be her.

But as she glanced down at herself, she realized she was without too many options at the moment seeing as that coward J.T. had run off and left her to fend for herself.

Unexpected tears pricked her eyes and she dashed them away, her finger coming away with a smudge of black. "Crap," she muttered, going to the mirror to fix her makeup. "No man is worth ruining your makeup for," she reminded herself with a slogan that she'd read in a magazine while waiting at the dentist's office for a new crown.

But the worst part was that J.T. had seemed like the kind of man who would go to the ends of the earth to protect his woman.

Well, you're obviously not his woman. Duh.

And she was okay with that, she countered stubbornly. "You didn't graduate top of your class to aspire to be some guy's *woman*."

The door opened and two men appeared—not the

same men who had transported her, but apparently Anso shopped at the same thug shop because they all seemed to share similar traits—and she followed with her head held high, holding on to her dignity with both hands.

If she ever saw J.T. again, she'd do two things: first, pop him in the mouth for leaving her and, two, kick him in the shins for putting her in the hands of a man who thought to make her his brainy harem girl!

Anso DeLeon was used to having things his way. He accepted no obstacles and that included excuses framed in the vernacular of an "environmental impact survey."

He also had no use for "moral" and "ethical" quandaries.

Not that he'd ever suffered any.

Ahhh, there she is. His prize. Dr. Hope Larsen. He rose and gave a subtle bow in deference to the radiant beauty standing warily before him and graced her with a benevolent smile. "You look ravishing," he said, and kissed her cool hand. "This look suits you."

"It's not exactly my style and not what I had in mind for a dinner invitation," she said, allowing him to seat her at the lavishly appointed table. Hope locked eyes with him, her keen mind and fiery spirit everything he'd thought they would be. "Are you going to tell me what's in store for me or do I have to guess?"

Anso chuckled and took his seat, amused. "You are not one for idle chatter. I like that. A woman who knows when to close her mouth is a rare treasure, indeed."

"Yes, well, as is a man who knows that women are not chattel and haven't been for quite some time now."

"You are naive if you believe that," he said evenly, pouring wine for them both. "Women will always be owned in some fashion as long as the men rule the world. But it does not have to be unpleasant for the woman. Some chains are desired, even sought after."

"Not by this woman," she returned with a steely glare that he found incredibly arousing. "I am a scientist, not some silly sorority girl who is wowed by your obscene show of wealth and this ridiculous gown… Sorry, but did you get this out of a porn star's closet? There is barely enough fabric to cover a baby, much less an adult."

He laughed at her scorn, his smile widening as his gaze roamed her curves and valleys, noting with pleasure how her nipples were clearly visible in the hand-chosen garment. "I find it most pleasing."

"I do not," Hope countered, her chin lifting in a mutinous gesture. "I'm not ashamed of my body, but I don't believe in showing it off to someone who hasn't earned the right to see it. And you, sir, have not earned that right. Nor will you *ever*." She drew a breath and continued, saying, "Let's get to the point. Why am I here?"

Anso smoothed his hair and smiled. "You know why. I have need of your particular skills. You alone can help me achieve what I desire most, which makes you the most important person in my universe right now. Does that not please you? Who in this world would do anything for you in exchange for what you are trained to do? You paint me as a villain, but I am simply a man—a businessman—who will do anything to see that my business thrives."

"Running me down like an animal isn't the best way to compel me to help you."

He shrugged. "I'm an impatient man. It is one of my faults. When your friend was…*averse* to helping me achieve my goals, I was not about to make the same mistake twice."

Hope's eyes glistened as she swallowed. "You killed my friend."

"Unfortunate," he agreed. "She, like you, had a brilliant mind. I weep for the loss we all suffer for her untimely end."

"Untimely? Yeah, I'll say. Funny how that happens when you end up shot on the street."

"The world is a dangerous place," he murmured as if they were simply discussing world events and not the most horrifying shock of her life.

Losing Tanya had been like losing her best friend. They'd started out as a colleagues, but had quickly turned into confidantes.

"You're a monster," she said, wiping at a tear as it tracked down her cheek. "I won't help you."

"Please, do not make a rush to judgment," he said, gesturing to the servants. "You are hungry and overwrought from your perilous journey. We will eat, enjoy each other's company and then perhaps we shall retire for more pleasurable pursuits before we talk business."

"I'm not going to sleep with you," she said point-blank. "So unless your pleasurable pursuits include reading quietly or playing backgammon, you'll just have to amuse yourself with one of your Brazilian blow-up dolls."

"Redheads have always fascinated me. Such fire, such spirit. I imagine you are a hellcat in bed. The thought pleases me greatly, but I am not one to force a woman. However, I feel you will come to seek me of your own accord. I can offer much to a woman like you. It would be my honor to shower you with your greatest desire. You would make fine sons. A woman such as you should be treated as the rarest treasure."

Hope balked at the mention of bearing his children. "S-sons? Listen, I don't know what kind of time warp you're stuck in, but I am not some baby factory and I definitely don't consider it an honor that you would like me to be your biological receptacle!" She pushed her chair back with indignant fury and stated in a low tone, "I've lost my appetite after all," before attempting to leave the room, but she was promptly returned to her seat with a rough push by his guards.

"You have much to learn, Dr. Hope Larsen, but I am eager to teach." He snapped his napkin and smoothed it over his lap, his appetite roaring as loudly as his libido. The servant placed a plate of rare steak exquisitely prepared with baby red potatoes in front of him and he inhaled the aroma with relish. He selected his knife and fork, addressing Hope as he cut into the bloody meat. "I am a man who is accustomed to having the best. The best chef in the world, the best architect for my castle, the best people in my employ. I am generous to those who are loyal to me and ruthless to those who betray me."

"And how do I play into all this? How did you know Tanya?"

"I've been very blessed to have many things work in my favor, but there is something that has stymied my every attempt to circumvent, and as you can imagine, it does not please me."

"Welcome to the real world. Can't always get your way."

"Perhaps for ordinary people that is true. Not for me."

"And what makes you special?"

"Money, Dr. Larsen. Lots and lots of it. I have more money than some small countries. And I put it to good use. However, there are some things that money cannot influence, much to my annoyance."

"Which would be?"

"There is an indigenous tribe deep within the Amazon, very difficult to find, very suspicious of Western influence. They shun all contact with modern civilization and defend their territory most vigorously."

"I guess it's hard to buy off people who don't deal in any concept of currency," she said with a smirk, which he allowed to slide. There would be time enough for correction later.

"Yes, indeed. And when the environmentalists discover that your company is trying to move the tribe out of their native land to a different section of the jungle, it's suddenly a crime against the Indigenous Culture Act."

"Well, it is," she agreed with open scorn for his dilemma. "An indigenous culture without any previous involvement with the outside world is protected. You can't do anything to them or their land." Suddenly, she paled. "But if they are to die due to natural causes…"

"The obstacle of the indigenous people would become moot."

Hope gasped and her hand went to her mouth as she processed his meaning. He smiled more widely at her quick reasoning. "You want the virus to kill the tribe in your way."

"I call it the Hand of God virus. Is there anything more perfect than a virus that can mimic any known pathogen in the world with deadly efficiency? Your brilliant mind solved the riddle and created deadly perfection. The Hand of God virus will remove the obstacles in my way and I will be free to move forward with my newest acquisition."

"You're insane if you think I'm going to help you destroy an entire tribe of innocent people." She looked aghast and disgusted at the same time. "You can't just eradicate an entire tribe of people because you want to make more money."

"Why not?"

She sputtered, "Because you can't! It's immoral, against all rules of nature and just plain wrong."

"You created the virus. Were you concerned with the application when you were pushing to find the missing links in the chain? No. You were hungry, driven to create something magnificent. The science aroused you in a way that you cannot deny. I understand that drive. I celebrate that quality in you. Where others would pass judgment, I admire your skill. We are not so different, you and I, Dr. Larsen."

He smiled at the sudden tears gathering at the corners of her eyes.

"We are nothing alike," she whispered.

"Lies do not become us. Only with truth can we accept who we truly are. The sooner you stop fighting your nature, the sooner you will find peace."

Anso sliced a piece of beef and slid it into his mouth, relishing every subtle flavor.

Winning was a delightful complement to aged Kobe beef.

12

AFTER THAT INTERMINABLY excruciating dinner, Hope was roughly returned to her quarters and the door locked soundly, leaving her to fret and stew in her own anxiety.

The easy path would be to dismiss Anso's words as nonsense spewed by a madman, but there was a glimmer of truth to his assessment.

Had there been a moment when she'd paused to think of the ramifications of the viral research and how it could be perverted if put into the wrong hands?

Yes.

A long moment.

She'd even broached the subject with Tanya, but her fears had been effectively shelved by Tanya's levelheaded approach to science.

"If we feared every potential misuse of technology or scientific advance, we'd still be crouched in caves wearing animal pelts. We have to move forward—it's in our biology to crave progress, to never remain satisfied with the status quo, and thank God for that. Imagine if Edward Jenner had been content to watch smallpox rip through communities. Because of his need to create a vaccine, we no longer fear one of the greatest childhood killers and I think that's pretty damn great."

Hard to argue with that logic. "True. But what we're trying to create? Sometimes it worries me that in the wrong hands...it could be devastating."

Tanya gently steadied Hope and said in all seriousness, "You have a good heart. We are so close to a breakthrough—it's normal to fear success and invent scary theories that could self-sabotage your own mind, but you are too brilliant to let something as silly as self-doubt ruin the single most important discovery in the twenty-first century. This is bigger than the internet, honey. I'm talking big."

Hope laughed. "Bigger than the internet?"

"Much."

Risking a smile, Hope said, "Well, I *am* excited about this new test batch. I think we're on the verge of breaking through."

"Just imagine that big fat bonus that's waiting for you when the first viable batch passes all protocols. Have you thought of what you're going to buy?"

Hope paused, realizing she hadn't given the bonus much thought, being too preoccupied with the project to consider the hefty bonus being offered for a successful trial. "Not really. I think I'll just put it in savings or a CD for retirement."

Tanya scoffed playfully. "That's no fun. You earned it. You need to whoop it up, go to Vegas, take a trip, buy something outrageously expensive and designer that looks ridiculous and that you can never wear anywhere but the streets of Paris or Milan. Something exciting!"

She laughed at the very idea. "No, thank you. I'm much more excited about the idea of not trying to exist solely on Social Security when I'm too old to work. How about you? As the supervisor, you get a bonus, too."

Tanya winked. "Oh, girl, that money is already spent. I have plans for that cash."

"Such as?"

She sighed happily. "I'm going to Mackinac Island in the Upper Peninsula of Michigan to spend the summer. I'm going to rent a beautiful beachside villa and spend the day reading and drinking iced tea with tiny finger sandwiches."

"You've got it all planned out, I see," Hope teased. "But why Michigan? Why not somewhere tropical?"

"I've always dreamed of going there. It's a beautiful place that's only occupied during the summer months and there are no cars allowed. It's relaxed and quaint and as far from stress as I can imagine. I can't wait."

Tanya's revelation was telling. She was a top-level researcher and supervisor for Tessara Pharm, and the stress level must've been atomic.

Hope roused herself from her memory, wiping at the stray tear that snaked down her cheek.

Tanya never got the opportunity to see Mackinac.

"Robbery gone wrong, my ass," she said bitterly. Anso had admitted that he was responsible for Tanya's death and he wasn't the least bit remorseful. But then, when you had the kind of money and power that Anso DeLeon had, remorse wasn't something that you had to feel.

Hope removed her ridiculous dress and tossed it to the floor with more force than necessary.

She went to the armoire and found more clothes hanging, all in her size. The fact that Anso had selected these outfits with her in mind made her skin crawl. She wasn't his scientist Barbie to dress up as he pleased. Eschewing the fine clothing, she climbed into the bed naked, preferring to be nude than to be dressed as Anso desired.

The small defiance was all she could muster at this point.

Exhausted, brokenhearted and defeated, she succumbed to a deep sleep gratefully.

At least in sleep, she could escape her reality for a brief moment.

13

J.T. KNEW THE plan was to sit and wait for backup, but it was easier said than done when all he could think of was Hope's stricken expression as he'd left her behind.

The darkness echoed around him with the sounds of the jungle and he knew it was madness to head back without reinforcements, but hell, why start making smart decisions now?

Because you have to start thinking with your damn head for once.

It was dark as a tomb. He couldn't see two feet in front of him. If he was hell-bent on heading back without Teagan, J.T. would still have to wait until first light so he didn't end up walking off a damn cliff.

It wasn't as if the Amazon came equipped with streetlamps to light the way.

So even if his strongest urge was to strike out with nothing more than grim determination and a fervent prayer, he was going to stay lashed to that damn tree until morning because the odds were already shit against him, and he wasn't about to make them worse.

Biting back his frustration, he tried to close his eyes and at least get some sleep, but that was a losing battle, too.

The biggest question still haunting him—the same question he should've demanded an answer to from the start—was probably the one thing that'd put them into this situation.

What the hell was she packing around?

He didn't care what it took this time around—he was going to find answers.

J.T. managed to steal a few fitful hours of sleep, but when the first milky ray of light dawned, he was out of the tree and heading back the way he'd come.

It wasn't hard to find his own trail from the broken branches through the virgin rain forest, and thankfully the rain had held off during the night, leaving his footprints visible in the soft muddy floor.

But as easy as it'd been to find his own footprints, he figured it was dumb luck that anyone sent after him hadn't also stumbled across the path.

Within an hour he was at the compound, surveying the layout. Guards patrolled the perimeter, but only a sparse crew, which made them fairly easy to circumvent.

He supposed whoever signed the checks in this massive place was feared enough to give a wide berth, thus the minimal guard presence.

Not to mention this place was creepy as hell with its overwhelming opulence tucked away in the middle of the rain forest.

It was the kind of place where one could imagine satanic rituals going on with sacrificed children and shit like that.

Good going—try to keep it positive, Carmichael.

He climbed the fence at a spot that was relatively hidden by trees, then dropped soundlessly to the manicured lawn, using the diminishing shadows for cover as he searched for a way into the fortress.

At the sound of approaching voices, J.T. ducked into an alcove, listening.

"Boss man likes that red-hair woman. She fine and all, but what's all the fuss for? She ain't nothing but an uppity bitch, as far as I can tell. And I know the best way to keep a woman like that in line."

"Watch it, Pacon," another growled in warning. "Keep your dick in your pants unless you want to find yourself without one. Boss is real particular about this one and I like my head where it's at. There ain't no woman worth dying for. Not even one as fine as that one."

Pacon shot back with a petulant whine. "All right, all right, I'm not going near her. What's she got in that pack, anyway? Boss man's got it under lock and key in some sort of freezer."

"Hell if I know and I don't care. Nothing good, I can tell you that. Now get back to your post."

The footsteps retreated and J.T. emerged cautiously. Chances were wherever Hope was being held was heavily guarded. He needed a gun.

J.T. mulled over the bit of intel. Whatever Hope had needed to be kept cold. Which meant that she must've been transporting it in a specialized case.

That was why she'd been so particular about her pack. There was no other way to carry what she had to the lab.

But what the hell was she carrying?

J.T. spied a window with a balcony above him. It wouldn't be easy, but he could climb the wall.

Fitting his fingers into the tiny slats, he grimaced as the pain of climbing using the strength of his fingers and toes ricocheted up his arms.

It'd been a long time since he'd been free-climbing.

And now he remembered why he didn't do it any longer.

None of that mattered.

Just climb.

Find Hope.

"You handsome SOB. What trouble are you into now?"

Teagan accepted the hearty slap on the back from his former Air Force special-ops buddy Kirk Addler while Harris McGoy and Ty Eden added their two cents, as well.

"You never call, you never write," Kirk drawled, his signature smart-ass quips delivered with a California-boy accent. He pulled Teagan into a manly embrace even as he gave him shit. "Let me guess—your ass is in a sling and you need us to patch up your boo-boo."

As happy as he was that his buddies had answered the all-call without hesitation, he didn't have time to shoot the breeze and trade wisecracks over a game of poker.

"I appreciate you guys showing up. I'm about to ask a doozy of a favor."

Harris, a short redheaded Irishman with a taste for fine whiskey and a good time, grinned and slapped his hands together, saying, "It's about bloody time. I'm bored out of my gourd with all this soft living. Retirement sucks."

Ty, the quieter of the bunch and arguably the smartest, waited for Teagan to finish.

"I'll cut to the chase. J.T. is stranded in South America, people are trying to kill him and there's no way I'm letting my little brother die in the Amazon jungle."

"What's the little bugger done this time?" Harris asked, amused. "Going quite afar for a little strange, don't you think?"

"It's not like that. He took on a client that turned out to be on the run from some very bad people and he got mixed up in it."

"Sounds like J.T.," Kirk agreed, not the least bit surprised. "Frankly, I don't know how that guy is still alive. He's always been riding the edge of safe and sane. That's what I liked most about him."

"Yeah, well, I can't pull him out alone and I know a few

of you still have connections that might make it easier to get in and get out without getting killed."

"What's the window?" Ty asked.

No sense in sugarcoating things. "Yesterday."

"For crying out loud," Harris grumbled, rolling his eyes. "Why don't you make it difficult or worth our while. I mean, for a second I thought you were going to ask us to rope the moon for you."

Teagan knew he was asking a lot. "I understand if you don't want to get involved. If it weren't J.T. in this mess, I'd walk away, too."

"Getting in and out shouldn't be a problem. We can fly low enough to stay under the radar. But something tells me you know that isn't the biggest obstacle."

"I have a lock on J.T.'s location, but he won't leave without his client."

"Is this about a woman?" Harris complained. "That boy can't keep his dick from getting him into trouble."

"It's complicated," Teagan said, not quite understanding J.T.'s situation enough to explain.

"It's never complicated with that boy," Harris grumbled. "He'll chase after any skirt, regardless of the consequences. Remember that time he tangled with his sergeant's daughter? I thought he was a goner for sure."

"To be fair, Bethany was hot enough to start a fire. Can't say I blame the kid," Kirk chimed in with a grin. "Whatever he had to suffer for her was, no doubt, worth it."

"Six weeks of small-space training," Teagan answered wryly. "Cured him of any claustrophobia, that's for sure."

"Yeah, total immersion therapy. But that's a bitch. You wouldn't find me crawling into no small coffin-like space." Harris shuddered.

They were getting off topic. Not unusual with this group, but time was ticking. "Be that as it may, he won't leave without her, so we have to rescue her, too." He eyed the guys. "Are you up for a completely unsanctioned mission with little to no reward aside from bragging rights when you're drunk?"

Kirk laughed. "You had me at *unsanctioned*. I have some vacation time I can cash in. How about you, Harris? Think you can spare a day or two for adventure?"

Harris scowled. "If you're in, I'm going. No way you're going to hang that over my head for the rest of my life. Besides, I could use a little excitement to remind me that I'm not dead yet."

Teagan laughed at the small Irishman. "Thirty-six is hardly one foot in the grave."

"Feels like it when you've been neutered and grounded."

"Honorably discharged with a medal or two," Kirk reminded Harris. "And look at the bright side—you might get shot or something. That would be exciting."

"When do we leave?" Ty asked, bringing the conversation back on point.

Teagan looked at his watch and answered. "We leave in fifteen. Plane is ready to go when we are."

Harris grumbled, "I'm grabbing snacks for the ride. God knows what kind of food situation we'll be in and none of you assholes are going to chow down on my leg if things go bad."

Kirk slapped Harris on the back as they walked to the kitchen area of the hangar. "Always looking on the positive side—that's what I like about you, McGoy."

"Shut up, you feckin' idiot."

Ty waited until they were clear of earshot and said to Teagan, "What's the real story?"

"I wish I knew. J.T. is in something big. It's not like him to put Blue Yonder at risk. Hell, he and I were fighting about letting the business go when he took on this client. He was all for sticking it out, while I was saying we ought to fold up shop. I can only assume there was the promise of a lot of cash, but even so, I can't see J.T. jumping into something without a good reason."

"I've got a contact at the embassy that can help us. She can hook us up with transportation and contacts within Brazil."

"Thanks, man."

It didn't matter if years had passed; the bond the four of them shared was something that could come only from the brotherhood of surviving some serious shit and vowing to always have each other's backs.

Even if it meant rescuing a little brother who was too hotheaded to see reason at times.

True to their training, within fifteen minutes they were saddled up and ready to roll.

"Hold on to your butts," Teagan advised. "We're about to ride straight into the mouth of hell."

"Wooooo-eeee!" Kirk yelled, pumping the air. "I love a mission with low odds of success!"

Teagan grinned and they took to the air.

Stay alive, J.T. We're coming.

14

HOPE STARED AT the tiny strip of cloth that masqueraded as a top and the matching linen pants that were, once again, completely see-through, and lost her temper.

"What the hell am I supposed to do with this?" she fumed, lifting the offensive outfit with disgust. She hated that Anso was delighting in dressing her up like his own personal plaything and she could do nothing to stop him.

It was either wear the clothes he provided or walk around stark nude—which she had a feeling Anso wouldn't mind in the least.

He was playing a strange game with her and she didn't understand the rules.

She wasn't accustomed to being judged by her looks. In her entire life, she'd never placed much value on such superficial things. In truth, she was a bit of a nerd, preferring to enjoy the quiet of the library or attend lectures on cellular function by leading experts in the field.

Dressing up was something she had to do for formal functions to impress donors. The social game had never been her strong suit.

Anso had her at a distinct disadvantage. Was she supposed to be coy and flirty to endear Anso to her side or would that only encourage him to take things to the next level, which he had already implied he was more than interested in doing?

She shuddered in revulsion at the idea of Anso touching her with so much as a pinkie finger, much less his entire body.

As much as she wanted to knock a tooth out of J.T.'s thick skull, she knew it would be a long time before she managed to scrub the memory of J.T.'s touch from her mind.

A pang of grief reminded her of his abandonment and she sniffed back the tingle in the back of her nose signifying that tears weren't far.

Hope wouldn't cry over him.

She barely knew him.

Sure, he'd saved her life twice, she'd saved his and they'd gone over a waterfall together, but she didn't even know what his favorite food was or the color of his eyes.

Not true.

His eyes were a hazel green, similar to her own, except his sparkled with just a hint of trouble that was incredibly appealing.

She sucked in a tight breath and exhaled with a slow deliberate motion. Now was not the time to wallow in the memories of the past. Two days ago was hardly the past, a snarky voice inside her head quipped, but she pushed all thoughts of J.T. away.

J.T. wasn't here to save the day. She had to save the day herself.

Except she had no idea how and she was woefully ill equipped to save herself, much less the day.

Hope lifted the tiny outfit and sighed with a resigned shake of her head.

Time to play dress up for the mad billionaire.

She supposed it was better to play his Barbie doll than

his scientist because God knew he had terrible plans in mind for that role.

Tugging on the tight clothing, she gasped as her breasts bulged out the top, and she couldn't help but grimace at the idea that she looked as though she were auditioning for the remake of *I Dream of Jeannie* as the linen pants clung to her hips and thighs, but flared at the ankle.

"I feel like an idiot," she grumbled, shaking her head. "I'm glad to see my education has served me well."

"I don't know—I think it holds a certain charm."

Hope gasped and whirled around to see J.T. emerge from her balcony with a strained grin.

Her first impulse was to jump into his arms, so grateful to see him, but then she remembered that he'd abandoned her and she stiffened with a scowl.

"What are you doing here?"

One dark eyebrow rose. "Um…rescuing you?" His gaze traveled her outfit, resting on her breasts, and she fought the urge to cover herself. "Although I gotta say…this is a bit confusing and arousing. Why are you dressed like that?"

"Like I would dress like this on my own," she hissed, flapping her arms and tugging at the diaphanous material with disgust. "He makes me dress like this. It's all part of his sick game."

His grin faded and his eyes darkened. "And just who is this person?"

Someone who wants me to help him commit mass genocide! But she couldn't exactly share that without going into further detail so she kept her answer closer to the surface.

"His name is Anso DeLeon. He's some billionaire with too much time and power. He's also crazy. He likes to dress me up like his own personal Barbie and it's degrading as hell, so stop looking at me like I'm something you want to eat."

"You do look delicious," he admitted with a regretful sigh, but switched to business quickly. "Look, we need to get you out of here and we don't have much time to do it."

"I can't leave without my pack," Hope said stubbornly. "I have to find out where he's hiding it first."

"Hope, we don't have a lot of time to mess around," he said, impatient. "I've got transport coming, but we have to get out of here first."

"I'm not leaving without my pack."

"You and that goddamn pack," he growled. "You willing to die for the stupid thing?"

She swallowed. "Yes. If it comes to that." Hope couldn't explain why. But it was her responsibility to make sure that no one was hurt by her research. And if that meant dying to do so, she was willing. Tanya had given her life; why wouldn't Hope? "But I don't want to die," she added quickly. "Let me find out where Anso is keeping my pack. In the meantime, you can hide here in my room until I get back."

He could tell she wasn't going to budge, which was a good thing. No sense in wasting energy on useless tasks. Hope risked a small smile. "Thanks for coming back for me."

"Of course. I told you I was coming back," he returned gruffly, and she wanted to kiss his scruffy cheek. She felt safer already, even if it was an illusion.

Footsteps sounded and she ushered him into the expansive closet with a "Shhhhh," seconds before her door opened and AnaMaria entered, gushing with praise as she gazed at Hope.

"Who knew hiding beneath those ugly tattered clothes was a beautiful, sexy goddess just waiting to emerge?"

A sexy goddess? Hope forced an awkward smile. How did one accept a compliment like that with any kind of grace? "Thank you," she said, trying not to squirm with embarrassment knowing that J.T. was listening to this ridiculous conversation. "So, do you know what the plans are for today?" she asked, hoping to get some useful information for J.T.

AnaMaria smiled. "The master has fun plans for you today. You're going to love becoming part of our family."

Good God, and no, she wouldn't. A moment of panic caused her to falter. "AnaMaria, you do realize I'm being held against my will, right?"

AnaMaria appeared confused. "Are you being mistreated? Are you not enjoying the master's hospitality?"

"Being held captive in a gilded cage doesn't make it any less of a cage," she explained gently when AnaMaria remained unable to comprehend why Hope was being difficult. "I don't want to be here and he won't let me leave. That's the definition of holding someone hostage."

"He is so generous to buy you such fine things," AnaMaria said, frowning with unhappiness at Hope's comment. "You are very lucky and ungrateful."

This conversation was going nowhere.

It was clear AnaMaria couldn't understand why Hope wanted to get the hell out of there. Hope had to remember that she and AnaMaria came from two different worlds. Perhaps compared to whatever place AnaMaria came from, this was a huge step up.

"I'm not used to this kind of lifestyle," she said, choosing her words carefully. "I don't know how to acclimate to my new surroundings. I guess I'm struggling."

At that AnaMaria smiled with dawning understanding. "When I first came, I was scared. But the master soon showed me that I had nothing to fear. He is a very smart man. And kind when you please him."

Hope wondered what happened to the people who displeased Anso.

"Perhaps you could give me a small hint as to what

is in store for me today?" Hope tried again with a small engaging smile. "I'm the kind of person who likes to be prepared."

But AnaMaria shook her head, adamant. "My job is to bring you to breakfast. We've already spent too much time talking. Come."

With a final backward glance, Hope followed AnaMaria out of her quarters and down the airy hallway to a beautiful open breakfast nook. The warm, humid air caressed her skin and the sultry scent of the Amazon jungle teased her senses. Under different circumstances, this compound could have doubled as a private resort.

But as she'd tried to tell AnaMaria, a cell with golden bars was still a prison.

Anso smiled with obvious pleasure when she entered the room, gesturing grandly for her to sit beside him. Hope gritted her teeth and took the seat that was offered, even though it was too close for her comfort.

Anso tapped his cheek and AnaMaria promptly kissed it. Hope wanted to vomit.

"Lovely girl, isn't she?" Anso remarked with a possessive gleam in his eye as he watched AnaMaria leave the room. "Obedient and exotic. A perfect Amazon bloom."

Gag me. Hope pinned Anso with a derisive look. "If you're expecting me to kiss your cheek like that poor, misguided girl, you're sadly mistaken. That will never happen."

Anso chuckled, snapping his linen napkin onto his lap. "I rescued her from her village. She was filthy, dressed in rags and destined to marry a man three times her age until I intervened."

"And how exactly did you do that?"

He shrugged with false modesty. "It was a relatively small thing. I simply offered her father more than the man she was supposed to marry."

"And what is the going rate for a young girl these days?"

"In AnaMaria's case, the cash equivalent of two donkeys, a goat and a pig. It was quite a bargain."

Hope didn't try to hide her disgust. "People should never be bought and sold."

"AnaMaria is not unhappy with her situation. In fact, she is quite grateful. I saved her from a life of misery that would've ended only with her death. Ask her. She will tell you herself how happy she is here with me."

Hope set her jaw. "Trading one type of slavery for another is no step up and you're wasting your breath trying to convince me otherwise. If you truly cared about her welfare, you would've sent her to school instead of setting her up in your household to serve you and call you master, which is deplorable, by the way. What you're doing is taking advantage of an ignorant girl who doesn't know any better. Don't try and package it any differently."

Anso chuckled. "Ahh, Dr. Larsen, your fire and passion appeal to me. Life will never be dull with your sharp tongue. You will come to me in your own time. I can wait. However, in the meantime, we will discuss business."

A new sort of dread filled Hope. "What sort of business?" Hope asked, being deliberately obtuse. "There is nothing that you and I have to discuss, as far as I'm concerned. Furthermore, where is my personal property? I expect my bag to be returned to me."

"The contents of your bag are being carefully taken care of. Let us enjoy breakfast. One cannot think properly without a good breakfast."

But Hope wasn't hungry. If anything, her stomach was in a constant state of panic. The sick game Anso was playing was much like a cat toying with a mouse.

And she was the mouse.

"I'm an American citizen. You cannot hold me here against my will."

"Tell me about the man you were traveling with," Anso commanded, redirecting the conversation. He sliced into a ripe papaya and savored the fleshy fruit. "Is he your lover?"

The flare of her cheeks probably gave her away, but she maintained stubbornly, "That's none of your business."

"Ah, so he is."

Hope seamed her lips shut. She did not want to talk about J.T. "My personal business is my own."

"Everything about you is my business. You belong to me. Have you not figured that out yet?"

Hope sputtered. "I do not belong to anyone. Just because you've closeted yourself up in this jungle fortress, surrounded by simpleminded girls who are wowed by your wealth, doesn't mean that I am snowed by your act. All the money in the world doesn't change the fact that what you're doing is illegal and immoral. And the first chance that I get, I'm going to take you down."

Anso narrowed his gaze, and for the first time he lost the benevolent mask he wore for her benefit. "Careful, Dr. Larsen. I find that women are much more malleable after they've tasted the kiss of a whip. I am not above punishing a woman to remind her of her place."

He wasn't bluffing. Hope sensed in her bones that he wouldn't hesitate to beat her if it suited his purpose. He had to keep her alive, but she could do her job with bruises just as well as dressed in finery.

That message came across loud and clear.

Mask back in place, Anso smiled. "Let me disabuse you of any fantasy you might have that your lover will come to save you. My men will find him and put a bullet in his head. If you care about him, you will pray that he abandoned you. Because I do not take lightly to anyone trying to take what belongs to me."

Hope shuddered with true fear knowing J.T. was hidden

in her bedroom. She had to believe that J.T. knew how to keep himself safe, but they were in the lion's den and at any moment could be eaten.

"He's not my lover, simply my pilot. If your idiot thugs hadn't tried to shoot my plane down, I wouldn't have been caught in the jungle with him. I was paying him to deliver me to my lab."

Anso wiped his mouth with a slick smile. "My mistake. You remind me that only fools make assumptions."

She returned his smile with a thin one of her own. "I hired him to do a job. So, there's no need to chase after him on my behalf."

"Indeed, but one must be thorough."

Hope covered the chill bouncing down her spine with a delicate shrug. "That's your concern. Mine is where you are holding my property. You are neither equipped nor qualified to handle what I was carrying."

Her answer seemed to mollify him. Brightening, he gestured toward her. "Please, eat. We have a full day ahead of us. I mustn't have the most brilliant gem in my collection lose her sparkle because she didn't eat her breakfast."

Eating was the last thing Hope wanted to do. And the idea of putting that food in her mouth made her physically ill. But she also knew that she needed to be able to think straight. And she couldn't do that if she had low blood sugar. Smothering her revulsion for Anso, she coolly picked up her fork and began eating. She needed to refuel if she was going to get herself out of this mess.

But she took a moment to privately pray that J.T. had figured out a plan that would get them both to safety.

Don't be a hero, J.T.

Don't get yourself killed for me.

15

FOLLOWING BREAKFAST, ANSO led Hope to a new part of the complex. It was obviously something that had only recently been finished, as it still smelled of new drywall and paint.

Anso was obviously quite pleased with the results, as he gestured with great flourish for her benefit, exclaiming, "Welcome to your new lab. I have spared no expense in ensuring that you have only the best to work with. Please, what do you think?"

Hope stared in utter incredulous shock. Tessara Pharmaceuticals never scrimped on value for their scientists, however, this lab was something out of a scientist's wet dream.

Of course, a madman with an endless stream of funds would be able to create the perfect setting to complete his genocidal dream.

She stared, words failing her. "And what exactly do you expect me to do here?"

"I have been following your research very closely. Although you and Ms. Fields had cracked the code to make the virus viable, you had not yet determined how to efficiently disseminate the virus."

"Because we never planned for it to be used in this

way!" she shot back, aghast. "The idea wasn't to create a weapon. There were supposed to be applications beyond destruction."

"Your naivety is endearing and annoying at the same time. Your company has military contracts. Scandal is Tessara's shadow. It is no secret that Tessara seeks out the most brilliant minds for their scientific foundation. Why do you think Tessara is so closely handfasted to your government? They have secrets worth protecting."

Hope stiffened. "I don't know what you're talking about. All I know is that I did not create this virus in order to kill an entire tribe of people!"

"Your concern is duly noted. Now, what else will you need to aerosolize the virus? I trust the lab is everything you will need?"

Hope could only gape. He truly believed she was going to do his bidding? She would rather die first. "You can make me wear these stupid outfits, but you can't make me help you kill people for your own gain."

"I find that beauty and brains are rarely found together. You, Dr. Larsen, are a delightful contradiction to my observation. However, while it distresses me to think of marring that beautiful skin of yours, one must remain on target with one's goals."

"And what's that supposed to mean?" she asked, feigning bravery. "You think that if you beat me, I'll become more open to genocide? Sorry, you'll have to kill me first."

Anso reached out to caress her cheek and she flinched away from his touch. His gaze narrowed. "I can only imagine that your stubbornness is a complement to your brilliance, but I do not have time for your childish show of emotion. I will give you one day to consider your options. After a little education, I feel you will change your mind."

At that Anso snapped his fingers and two hard-faced

men shaped like gorillas on steroids appeared in ill-fitting white suits.

"Take her to the education room. I will be there shortly," were his instructions and Hope was dragged kicking and screaming from that beautiful, deadly lab. Calling after her, he said, "Remember, there is no shame in begging for forgiveness, my brilliant dove. I await those sweet words from your beautiful lips."

Hope had no idea what an *education room* was, but she had a terrible feeling she had no wish to learn what Anso sought to teach.

J.T., help me!

J.T. WASN'T ABOUT to hang around in a closet all day. What he could tell about the house was that it was big enough to get lost in, but that also meant that there were plenty of empty rooms to duck into if needed.

Talk about a security risk. Whoever this Anso character was hiring for security should've been fired.

But that worked in J.T.'s favor and for that he was grateful.

He shimmied down the wall from the balcony and landed with a soft thud on the grass. He rounded the building, sticking to the walls, making his way carefully around the perimeter, learning the layout as best he could.

A shrill scream sent cold fear down his spine and he bolted in its direction.

If anything happened to Hope, he'd tear people apart with his bare hands.

HOPE WAS DRAGGED down a corridor as if she weighed nothing even as she struggled and kicked and screamed her head off the entire way.

"Let me go, you big idiot!" she yelled without effect.

"What you're doing is illegal where I come from and I'm certain it's illegal here, too!"

Rage, fear and panic fueled her muscles as she fought with everything in her to get free. She'd almost managed to wrangle herself loose when she was flung inside a room and the door closed. The two men, their impassive faces hewn from granite, advanced without mercy. She tried to run away, but there was nowhere to go.

Trapped like an animal, she was handcuffed and then hung from a hook in the center of the room, her feet barely able to take the pressure off her wrists. It was instant agony and she had to stand on tiptoe to relieve the pain.

The room was filled with horrifying contraptions. Seemed Anso had a thing for torture.

Tears filled her eyes as cowardice filled her heart.

What was Anso going to do to her?

It was easy to be brave when you were spewing hot words, but when push came to shove and the white-hot brand was nearing your skin? All bravado fled, leaving fear and desperation in its wake.

But she couldn't do what Anso wanted.

He was a despicable monster.

He was the reason Tanya was dead.

She'd refused him and paid the price.

Anso had no reservation about killing those who got in his way.

The door reopened and Anso entered with an expression that was determined yet pleasant, which made it all the more disturbing.

This was what a sociopath looked like, she realized.

Anso came to her and lovingly ran his hands down her sides, pausing on her hips. "You have a lovely figure. So womanly, so lush and yet lean. Again, the contradictions of Dr. Larsen intrigue me."

"What are you doing?" she asked, her voice trembling.

Cold sweat ran down the small of her back in spite of the heat in the room.

Anso gestured to his men and they responded by placing a long black leather whip in his awaiting hand. "You see, sometimes a strong woman, like a unbroken horse, must be tamed, must be taught how to properly respond to her master."

"You're not my master," Hope bit out, hating the tears rolling down her cheeks because they made her feel weak. "You're nothing but a rich sociopath with a God complex. That makes you the master of *nothing*."

He caressed her cheek with the butt of the whip. "You remind me of another. She, too, was as stubborn as she was beautiful. Pray you do not follow in her footsteps." He continued, walking a slow circle around her, taking his time. "I blame her youth. She did not possess the necessary maturity to understand when she was clearly bested. You, Dr. Larsen, are a very smart woman. I believe it will not take much to educate you on how to act."

Anso paused, then smiled.

"However, I will give you some time to think before your education begins. I believe you will come to the right decision."

"Which is what?"

He lost his smile. "To do as you're told."

Hope started to tell him to go screw himself, but a latent sense of survival curbed her tongue. She wasn't exactly in a position to be sassy and she didn't doubt that he wouldn't hesitate to beat her if given the chance.

Anso snapped his fingers and his thugs followed him out of the room, leaving Hope to hang painfully, her wrists screaming.

Her fingers were already going numb, her toes cramping. This was medieval torture. Blinking back tears, she willed herself to remain strong, but she knew everyone had a breaking point.

And let's face it—she wasn't a trained spy or anything like that.

She was a scientist, for crying out loud. Her most challenging physical test of endurance had been a Tough Mudder and she'd sworn to never do that again after getting mildly electrocuted on the course.

Hope thought of Tanya and swallowed her fear. Tanya had given her life. If that was what it came down to, to protect the world from what she'd created, that was her penance.

Just as her fingers lost all feeling and the cramp in her arch had become excruciating, the door opened and J.T. slid in silently, closing the door behind him and locking it with deliberate care.

Immediate tears sprang to her eyes as J.T. rushed to help her off that horrible hook, relieving the pressure on her wrists and toes.

She shuddered as he sheltered her in his arms, holding her tight.

"You get yourself in the most damnable situations," he joked in a strained voice as she quaked with silent tears, so grateful that he was there. "C'mon, let's get those cuffs off you, I Dream of Jeannie."

A watery chuckle escaped Hope as he helped her stand and she winced, as the pain in her feet hadn't quite subsided. J.T. found the keys to the cuffs and released her, then rubbed the circulation back into her abused hands.

Agonizing tingles and sparks flooded her fingers as the blood rushed to the digits, but Hope bit back the cry of pain as she weathered the inevitable process, knowing it needed to happen.

"I'm going to kill that bastard," J.T. said, rubbing the

redness on her wrists gently. "I'm going to put a bullet right between his eyes and not feel a moment's guilt doing it."

J.T. lifted her wrist to his lips and pressed a sweet kiss to her skin and she nearly sobbed with a breaking sort of emotion that was as foreign as it was all-encompassing, but they didn't have time to examine it—they both felt the ticking clock.

"Can you walk?" he asked and she nodded, knowing they had to get out of there now before they were discovered.

He slipped his hand in hers and took the lead as they wound their way out of the house, using stealth and cunning to evade the guards who milled around.

They cleared the house using a back entrance and J.T. helped her up and over the fence, then made quick work of climbing over to join her on the other side.

She stared helplessly at the fortress where her pack remained and J.T. knew where her mind had gone.

"I will come back and get your damn pack, but for now, we need to get the hell out of here while we still can."

Hope nodded, knowing their options were slim if they wanted to survive to see another day. She also knew that J.T. would keep his word. If he promised he would return, he would.

Satisfied, J.T. gripped her hand and they fled into the rain forest, putting as much distance as they could between themselves and Anso's long reach.

Frankly, Hope didn't think they could run fast or far enough. Anso was the great savior around these parts. How could they possibly find anyone who would help them get her pack and kill the charismatic lunatic?

Problems for another moment.

For now, they had to survive the rain forest.

Again.

16

J.T. HAD TO keep his head on straight, but he was still see-ing red.

He was going to kill that bastard for what he'd done to Hope.

Hope stumbled and went to the soggy ground, ripping the flimsy material of her genie pants.

"Ouch!" she cried out, frustrated as he helped her back to her feet. "This stupid outfit is beyond ludicrous." She wiped the mud from her knees and shook off her hands. "I feel like an idiot."

"If we weren't in mortal danger, I'd help you out of that outfit," he said in a silky tone as he pulled her into his arms for a searing kiss that was inappropriate given the situation, but he didn't he care. Hell, if he was going to die, this wasn't a bad way to go.

Sealing his mouth to hers, he let his fear and rage co-alesce into something white-hot as Hope clung to him, meeting the plunge of his tongue with a parry of her own.

"Should we be doing this?" she managed to ask, breath-less. "I mean…this is probably not the time. I mean, not that I'm not enjoying it, because I am, but this is sort of like those movies where people start making out when they are clearly not out of danger yet."

"Always gotta be the voice of reason, don't you?" he teased gruffly, but she was right. He reluctantly turned her loose and they struck out again, pushing through the dense foliage until they were far enough away for J.T. to make a phone call safely.

Hope bracketed her waist as she drew harsh breaths from running, cheeks flushed and hair flying every which way. She looked like a crazy person—and had never looked sexier.

Deliberately cutting his gaze so he could concentrate, J.T. called Teagan, but got his voice mail, which meant Teagan was still on his way, and that was a good sign.

"Teagan will use the GPS on my phone to find us. We just have to hole up and stay safe until he does."

"Anso will be looking for us," Hope said, worried. "How are we supposed to hide out until then?"

"We'll have to. It's our only choice. We can't trust anyone right now. Our best bet is to remain in the forest."

"With the snakes and bugs and mercenaries?" Hope groaned when he nodded. "Fabulous. Well, I suppose that's a step up from what Anso had in store for me by way of my *education*."

"Education?"

"Yeah. That's what he called it. He was going to whip me into submission. Apparently, that's his thing. I was not looking forward to the prospect of being beaten."

"What a sick prick."

Hope shuddered at the memory, still too fresh. "Yeah, you don't know the half of it."

J.T.'s expression sobered and by the set of his jaw she knew what was coming and she didn't blame him when he said, "It's about time you tell me what the hell is so special about that pack of yours."

J.T. was right. At this point he'd more than earned the right to know what he was risking life and limb for.

Time to come clean. "I've wanted to tell you, but I couldn't find the right words. And then after everything... I didn't want you to judge me."

"Why would I judge you?"

Hope drew a deep, fortifying breath and met his gaze bravely. "I work in the virology department of Tessara Pharmaceuticals. My supervisor, Tanya, and I managed to create the single most devastating virus in the twenty-first century. It has the power to mimic any known pathogen introduced to it."

J.T. did a double take, trying to absorb what she'd just revealed. "Wait a minute—are you telling me that this virus of yours can suddenly become, like, Ebola or the plague or smallpox?"

"Yes."

He stared, incredulous. "That's what you've been *protecting* this whole time? Why the hell would you create something like that? That's nuts, creating something so dangerous."

The very thing she'd been afraid of happening was unfolding right before her eyes and she couldn't help the defensive tone that flowed from her mouth. "There are other applications aside from destruction and that's what we were looking for. If it has the power to mimic any pathogen, then we were one step away from finding a way for it to mimic powerful cancer-fighting bacteria. Imagine if we could design a virus that would act as a warrior against disease, going after it with single-minded purpose. If we could do that, we could wipe out cancer, sickness, pretty much put a stop to anything aside from aging that could affect a human being's quality of life."

"Yeah, but you had to know that when word of that

lab bomb got out, you were going to have unscrupulous people—such as Anso DeLeon—coming after you."

"No, we didn't think of that," Hope admitted, facing his censure with a lifted chin. "Anso accused me of being naive and maybe I was. Tanya and I were too excited about our research and the breakthroughs to look at the potential ramifications. I'm sorry, but if you want me to be honest, that's the truth of it. Am I aware now that it was a mistake? Hell yes. But it's hard to explain to someone who couldn't possibly understand what it felt like to be on the verge of a discovery like this. It's intoxicating."

His mind was blown, she could tell, but she needed to come completely clean if they were going to move forward.

"Anso wanted the virus to wipe out a tribal village standing in his way of a development in the Amazon. I refused to do it."

"And how was he going to make you do that? Make the tribe drink your virus or something?"

She shook her head. "The virus had to be turned into an aerosol for the most effective way of distribution, and he set up this entire state-of-the-art lab for me to do this. I wasn't going to do it. Which is why he was going to *educate* me in the reasons why I should cooperate." Then she admitted her shameful fear. "If you hadn't shown up when you did…I might've caved and done what he wanted. I was so afraid."

Even though he was struggling with her revelation, he pulled her to him. "Most people would've been pissing themselves. You were brave. Don't ever forget that."

Hope didn't deserve his praise, but she sank into him, inhaling the spicy scent of his body, feeling safer in that moment than if she'd been tucked away in a panic room built with thick steel walls.

J.T. held her for a long moment and then after a brief kiss on her crown, he drew her away to return to the most pressing issue aside from survival, saying, "Okay, so we're back to the original question…what the hell are you going to do with that virus now? You have to destroy it."

That was the crux of it.

"That virus is my life's work. It's what Tanya died for. I can't just toss it in the trash. Besides, it's not mine to destroy. That's why I was taking it to the South American lab. Tanya and I thought it would be safer there. More contained."

"Are you sure Anso was the only one who was after the virus?"

She frowned. "I think so. Why?"

"How would he have known about your work? It's top secret, right?"

Hope nodded, getting where he was going. "Anso had said that he'd been watching my research for a while. Someone on the inside had to be feeding him updates."

"So that means whoever your mole is…is likely still embedded in your circle. Who has access to your files?"

"I don't know. Probably only the higher administrators in our department. Tanya was my supervisor, but I imagine her supervisor had access to our research docs."

"And who is that?"

Hope shook her head. "No, it can't be her. She's been with the company for years. She'd never do something so dirty."

"What's her name? My buddy Ty has some friends in IT who can dig around in her background and see what pops up."

"Deirdre Ellison, but we can't go digging into her life. What if we're wrong and we just violated her privacy for nothing?"

"And what if we're right?" J.T. tossed in as tension returned to her gut at the possibility of Deirdre's involvement. "If there is someone on the inside, you're still not safe and neither is that virus. Can you destroy it any other way?"

"It has to be destroyed in a specialized lab with heat and pressure. It's too dangerous to try it on our own."

"We'll figure it out." He cupped her face as he sealed his mouth to hers. She drank in his kiss, losing herself for a brief moment in the stolen pleasure. Their tongues tangled almost desperately, but there was a sweetness to it, too. J.T. had quickly become someone she needed, not only for her safety, but something deeper that she wasn't ready to examine.

Clinging to one another, J.T. broke the kiss and she was reluctant to let him go, but she knew now was not the time.

Had it been only days that they'd known each other?

Days that felt like a lifetime.

Of course, that wasn't good.

But it felt like heaven.

17

J.T. HEARD THE low-flying aircraft and immediately tensed, but when he scanned the plane and saw the familiar underbelly gliding below radar, he grinned from ear to ear.

Teagan!

God, he loved his brother.

He gently shook Hope awake and she came to with a start. "What is it?"

He pointed to the sky with a grin. "Reinforcements have arrived." J.T. climbed to his feet and helped Hope to hers. "C'mon, we have to follow. Teagan will have to land in a clearing and chances are if we heard the plane, so did Anso's thugs."

They followed the plane's trajectory and found the small plane in a clearing that was barely noticeable unless by air.

Teagan powered down the plane and as the blades slowly whirred to a stop, the door opened and Kirk, Harris, Ty and lastly Teagan erupted from the plane.

J.T. ran straight to Teagan and embraced him, too happy to see his brother to care about appearances.

"You're a sight for sore eyes, man. I wasn't sure you'd make it," he admitted.

"Like I would leave my little brother stranded in the

Amazon. If I didn't leave your busted ass in Afghanistan, I'm sure as hell not leaving you here with the bugs and snakes." Then Teagan's gaze traveled to Hope, who stood off to the side with a forlorn expression, clearly uncomfortable. "And you must be this mysterious client that's gotten my brother's tail in a twist." He reached out to shake Hope's hand. "Teagan Carmichael. Pleasure."

"The pleasure is mine," she murmured, shooting J.T. an uncertain glance. "Thank you for coming to save us."

J.T. knew it was too much to hope that the guys wouldn't remark on Hope's attire, but when Harris couldn't stop staring, J.T. couldn't help the scowl.

"Keep your eyes in your head, you dirty Irishman," J.T. growled, and Teagan just laughed and clapped him on the shoulder.

"Calm down." He motioned to Hope. "Let's get you guys out of here."

But Hope shook her head, saying before J.T. could explain, "We can't leave without my package."

"Is it a pile of money?" Kirk asked, his eyes lighting up with hope. "Or maybe some precious yet ultimately cursed diamond that we'll have to sell on the black market before we die from some unfortunate accident caused by the spirit who cursed the gem?"

Harris rolled his eyes. "You daft idiot. You've watched too much television. There's no such thing as curses."

"You're Irish! Superstition is part of your culture, man," Kirk protested as if Harris were betraying his own people. "You know, fairies and goblins and shit like that."

"Oh, good grief, we're not all superstitious fools. We all don't believe in a pot of gold at the end of the rainbow, neither. We do, however, believe in the power of fine whiskey and a woman's warmth, two things I'll be needing after spending time with you idiots, getting eaten up by blasted mosquitoes the size of lemons." Harris slapped his neck, wiping away bug guts. "See? Damn bastards could cart off a small child. I hate the rain forest."

J.T. couldn't help the weary smile. Through all the shit, humor had always been their saving grace. Good times.

It was Ty who spoke up as the voice of reason. "We need recon before we go charging into a hostile situation."

"His name is Anso DeLeon, a man who is both feared and celebrated around here. We don't know who to trust. The last person we trusted practically hand-delivered us to Anso without a second thought as he was counting his wad of cash."

"You always did have an eye for the troublemakers," Kirk teased, punching J.T. in the arm, adding with a wink, "Not that I blame you."

Hope blushed and J.T. wanted to grasp her hand as a show of support, but that would only encourage further ribbing, and right now they needed to focus.

Teagan agreed with Ty. "We can't go guns blazing into an unknown situation. We need to hole up, regroup and form a plan. We've got a contact at the embassy who can help us out. C'mon, let's do this smart and live to talk about it over beers later."

J.T. rubbed at the grit in his eyes knowing Teagan was right. He looked to Hope. "We will return for your pack, but Teagan is right—we have to be smart if we're going to have a snowball's chance in hell of succeeding."

"Okay," she agreed, her voice trembling. "Promise?"

"Promise."

They climbed into the plane as Harris quipped, "You look like shit. And smell just as bad. You're like a weapon of mass destruction. Damn, you could scare off wildlife with that stench."

Hope's small giggle loosened the tightness in his chest, but there were bigger problems up ahead and even more troublesome questions.

The burden of knowing what exactly they were going after hadn't made things less complicated—if anything, the knowledge made for a heavier burden, but he didn't regret Hope's telling him.

He didn't like the idea of her shouldering the entire weight by herself.

Even if she had created the problem.

If anything happened to Hope... *Don't go there.*

It was hard not to.

Somehow Hope had become more than just a client.

He could smell her on his body, could remember the taste of her kiss. She was seared into his synapses with the heat of their explosive chemistry.

It wasn't as if Hope was looking for attachments any more than he was, and frankly, they were about as ill suited as a giraffe and a lion. He was a maverick, a player. She was a scientist with a brain that he couldn't possibly fathom.

But together they made magic.

Hell yes, together they were a symphony of sensation and that was hard to ignore, but something warned that it was more than simply sexual chemistry that made their attraction white-hot.

But he didn't want to think about that. No, he had enough on his plate trying to keep her stubborn ass alive without taking a dirt nap himself.

"So, what do you think of Brazil?" Kirk asked with a smirk. "I hear the ladies are exotic."

A weary grin found J.T.'s lips. "If we manage to survive the next twenty-four hours, be my guest to find out."

All he cared about was Hope.

She was all the exotic he could handle.

TEAGAN MANAGED TO find a small, nondescript hotel for them through a military contact and they settled in for the night with plans to visit Ty's contact at the embassy first thing in the morning.

But first Teagan pulled J.T. aside for a private moment.

"So, what's really going on?" Teagan asked.

J.T. understood why Hope had been reluctant to share information about the virus. He also could see why it was wise to keep that information close to the vest. When J.T. didn't immediately start sharing intel, Teagan added his own two cents.

"You know, I did some digging around on that lab of hers. Tessara has a reputation."

"Yeah? Of what?"

"Being shady."

"It's a pharmaceutical lab. That's like saying politicians aren't truthful."

"A few years back I remember some talk about an experimental drug that had the power to wipe memory."

"No kidding?"

"Yeah. Real classified shit. Military grade. But it was hushed up pretty quick. Ty wasn't able to find much more information. My point being Tessara has a reputation for being involved with real dangerous stuff."

J.T. didn't question Teagan's intel. It certainly jibed with what Hope had already shared, though he wondered if she knew just how dangerous Tessara really was.

"If that's the case, then I trust that if she says she has to get to her lab, then she's not telling stories."

"You don't know her at all. What if she's not on the right side of things?"

He didn't want to think that of Hope, but he couldn't deny that his brother brought up a good point.

He knew next to nothing about Hope in the big scheme of things.

But his gut told him Hope wasn't a bad person. He was a good judge of character and his judgment had never let him down before, so he was going to have to trust that he was right about Hope.

"I trust her," J.T. said simply, letting the truth of his feelings do the talking. "Win or lose…I have to help her do what she came to do. Are you with me?"

Teagan shook his head as if J.T. had uttered nonsense. "Of course I am. I just wanted to get the lay of the land before we head out."

"Low odds for success," J.T. murmured with a half grin. "Still interested?"

Teagan exhaled as if there was no turning back, because there wasn't. "Civilian life was boring, anyway." He punched J.T. in the shoulder with a grin. "Now go spend some time with your woman. Lord knows, tomorrow isn't promised."

Amen to that.

When J.T. returned to the tiny hotel room he found Hope staring out the window, nervous and on edge.

"Is everything okay?"

"As okay as it can be."

"Your brother doesn't like me, does he?"

"He doesn't know you."

Hope nibbled her fingernail. "I don't blame him. I wouldn't like me either if I'd gotten my family member into deep doo-doo."

"'Deep doo-doo'?" he repeated, laughing. "Such language, Dr. Larsen. You kiss your mother with that potty mouth?"

Hope smiled nervously, still agitated. Didn't he realize maybe there was more going through her head than the situation facing them with the virus?

They were alone in a hotel room, the bed suddenly looming.

And suddenly it felt awkward between them, as if they

were teenagers dancing around the attraction they had for each another, unsure of how to act.

"Did it just get weird?" J.T. asked, half joking to lessen the tension. "I could room with my brother and the guys if you want the room to yourself."

"No," she said quickly. "I definitely don't want that. I feel safer with you around."

"I'm flattered," he said with a slight puff of his chest, but there remained an uncertainty, which she could understand. What was happening between them? J.T. decided to tackle the situation head-on. "Look, I get it. Extreme situations and all that. I'm not expecting a relationship when we get back to the States. We're not exactly peas in a pod."

Hope took a mental step back. Was she projecting a fear of a nonexistent future with J.T.? "No, not exactly," she agreed softly. But was that truly what was causing the tension? Or was it that she craved his touch with a ferocity that defied an easy explanation? She met his gaze with a crooked smile. "I'm glad we are on the same page."

"Yeah."

She twisted a lock of hair, realizing how grimy she was. Harris had been right. They both could use a scrub. J.T. more so than her, but she'd die before admitting that J.T.'s manly odor was intensely arousing. "Would you like to shower first?" she offered, trying to be solicitous when in fact she wanted to bury her nose in his chest and lick him clean.

Her cheeks flared with heat and she hoped to God J.T. wasn't so in tune with her facial expressions that he read her mind, because heaven help her, that was all she needed right now.

But when J.T. strode toward her, invading her personal space with delicious intent written all over his expression, her knees buckled as he said, "I think we should conserve water and shower together."

"Together?" she squeaked, immediately flushing with warmth. "Is that wise?"

"Darlin', we haven't done a single wise thing since coming into contact with one another—why start now?"

"You may have a point," she admitted with a hungry whisper, looping her arms around his neck and jumping into his arms. As he clasped her tight, she bit back a moan as the flat of his palm curved her behind with a possessive squeeze. There was something so incredibly virile and primal about J.T. that she couldn't rightly think straight when he touched her. He was the antithesis of every other man who'd ever touched her intimately and the thrill left her quite senseless.

A hungry kiss stole her breath and within minutes they were naked, writhing against each another, mindless of the grime and the sweat and mud caked on their bodies.

J.T. pushed her against the wall and knelt at her feet, drawing her to him so he could feast between her legs.

Threading her fingers through his hair, she lifted her hips, dying with pleasure as J.T. sucked and licked, spreading her to his marauding tongue.

Her knees quaked as her building climax approached rapidly, leaving her breathless and unable to speak as she exploded. But he gave her no moment to collect herself and the beautiful savagery of his total need for her was intensely arousing.

Turning her, he pushed apart her legs and held her to the wall as he entered her from behind, lifting her on her toes with each powerful thrust.

Being taken like this made her mindless with the pleasure as he pounded into her mercilessly, as if he were trying to drive out every bad memory with the force of his cock.

Hope shuddered as tiny mewls escaped her parted lips,

her nipples abrading against the faded wallpaper of the dingy bathroom.

"Hope," he gritted, her name like a prayer that he couldn't stop uttering. "*Oh, my G-God*, Hope!"

And then she shattered again, losing herself to the power of another epic orgasm the likes of which she'd never known.

She might've blacked out because for a long blissful moment, she knew only the sensations rocketing through her nerve endings, clenching her womb and causing every muscle to contract in unison.

Hope could've been orbiting the moon and she wouldn't have known.

All that existed was J.T. buried inside her.

And that was all she needed.

J.T. HELD HOPE while she slept, the scratchy bedding a welcome blessing after spending so much time in the rain forest.

He should've been exhausted after everything they'd done. Hell, the walls had proven thin, as one of the guys had banged on the wall after their third go-round.

He was going to catch hell tomorrow, he thought with a smile.

But even that entertaining thought faded when his stubborn brain returned to what was keeping him awake.

Hope had created a virus capable of knocking out the human race.

Yeah, it bothered him.

The saving grace was that she was trying to destroy it.

Which brought him to his next point of concern.

There was no way in hell Hope was going to stay put while he and the guys raided Anso's compound, and he didn't want her anywhere near that place or that sociopath.

But he knew how that conversation was going to go.

He would say, "Hope, I want you to stay behind, safe in this hotel."

And she would respond with a flat, "No."

And that was about how productive it would go because she was as stubborn as she was beautiful.

He tightened his hold around her and she shifted with a sigh in her sleep, blissfully unaware of his turmoil.

Like it or not, Hope was in his blood.

She was his virus.

Infecting him with something he couldn't quite shake.

He'd never get enough of her. Never kiss her hard enough, love her long enough or taste her enough times to get her out of his system.

That's a real problem, Carmichael, a voice quipped.

Yeah, thanks, Mr. Obvious. You're no help, so shut up.

It would all come down to what they found out tomorrow.

Hell, maybe none of them were destined to survive this round.

Comforting, he said to himself sourly.

You ought to write motivational speeches for children. Just go to sleep.

Everything would end as it would end.

No matter what he had to say about it.

J.T. lightly kissed Hope and she turned to him in her sleep, sighing like a sleepy kitten, and he knew there was no hope for him.

She owned him.

Whether she knew it or not.

18

MORNING BROKE WITH a drizzly rain, which seemed fitting seeing as Hope's spirits were dragging. It seemed an impossibility that they'd be able to breach Anso's compound without dying and the more she thought about it, the more she knew they were doomed from the start.

But J.T. wasn't about to let her give up.

"When the chips are down, that's when you find out what you're made of," he said, chucking her chin with a grin, but she couldn't appreciate his sentiment and simply looked away.

"Hey, what's wrong?" he asked.

"You mean aside from the obvious?" she replied in a lowered tone so their conversation didn't reach the others. "This is crazy. We're not going to make it out of that compound alive."

"Ye of little faith."

She exhaled a breath of frustration. "Will you stop joking around? This is serious. I don't want you to die over this. I couldn't handle it."

It was as much of an admission of her feelings as she would allow right now, but he seemed to understand.

J.T. pulled her close and whispered for her ears only.

"This ragtag bunch of guys may seem like a bunch of wisecracking idiots, but they're the most dangerous, most well-trained bastards the military ever churned out. Trust me—if anyone can get in and out of that compound, it's them. I wouldn't entrust your safety with anyone else."

Hope's gaze traveled to Harris, the short, blustery Irishman, who was bickering with Kirk, and then the more serious Ty, who was conferring with Teagan, and she suddenly saw them in a different light.

They were dangerous. Lurking beneath the surface of those handsome, rugged faces were men who knew how to get a job done—by whatever method necessary.

She turned to J.T., recognizing the same quality.

"Why did you retire out of the Air Force?" she asked quietly, wondering if he'd be truthful.

"I was becoming someone I didn't want to be," he answered, and she left it at that. She could infer any sort of conclusion about his answer, but honestly, she didn't need or care to know details.

All that mattered was that he was on her side.

And so were his friends.

"I have an eidetic memory," Hope told J.T., needing to show him that she could be helpful and not just a burden to the team. "I remember everything about the lab, including the code Anso punched in to enter. You're going to need me to get the pack."

J.T. eyed her with respect and a little awe. "Something tells me it's a bitch to play trivia games with you."

"I never lose," she admitted with a cocky grin. "Let me know when you want to get your ass kicked."

Laughing, he sneaked a quick kiss and she didn't mind in the least.

"So who the hell are we talking about?" J.T. asked, impatient to know who they were up against. "Who is this guy and why is everyone so afraid of him?"

Camille Jackson, the contact at the embassy, frowned. "You certainly tangled with the wrong person. He is universally loved and feared. The man has a lot of money and he uses it to donate to schools, as well as sponsor much-needed items for the police. Not to mention there isn't a woman in Brazil who wouldn't give a kidney to become his wife."

J.T. didn't care if the man shit gold bricks. "That man is up to no good. He kidnapped Hope. He tried to shoot us out of the sky. The man is dangerous. I don't care if there's a statue erected in his honor in the town square— the man is bad news."

"Doesn't sound like we're going to get much help from the locals," Teagan said.

Camille agreed with a worried expression. "On the surface he seems the benevolent benefactor. However, there are horrific stories about Anso DeLeon that aren't so savory. The problem is proving them. The man has more money than God. I don't know how you're going to go about this without ruffling a lot of feathers or, frankly, ending up at the bottom of a hole."

Teagan steadied J.T. with a reassuring hand. "We're not giving up. We'll find a way."

"So, what do we do?" He looked to Teagan. "I'm out of ideas."

But it was Camille who provided the first lead in a dead-end situation.

She lowered her voice. "It won't be easy when everyone sings the man's praises. But I do know someone who had an unfortunate run-in with Anso DeLeon. If there's anyone who would be willing to help you, it's him."

Camille scribbled the name and address on a piece of paper and slid it across the table to J.T. "This man came to me last year saying that his daughter had been taken by Anso and she never returned. He went to the police, but they wouldn't help him. There was no way they were going to bite the hand that fed them. Unfortunately, there was nothing I could do for him, either. But the man has no love for Anso DeLeon and I'm sure he would jump at the chance to finally find out what happened to his daughter."

J.T. shared a look with Hope as he accepted the slip of paper with gratitude. He couldn't imagine a father's pain in losing his daughter without answers and suspecting who was responsible and being unable to do anything about it.

"Thank you. I appreciate your help," J.T. said, shaking her hand. "Why did the man come to the embassy for help? Is he a US citizen?"

Camille shook her head, sadness creeping into her eyes. "He came to me because he and I were dating at the time. After the police refused to help him, he turned to me in desperation. I couldn't help, either. Eventually, the strain killed our relationship. But he is a good man and I truly hope he finds his daughter, or at least finds the answers."

"That's awful," Hope murmured with empathy. "Thank you for helping us."

J.T. nodded. "We appreciate all you've done to help. I know you're probably taking a risk."

Camille nodded. "Best of luck. I'm sorry I couldn't do more."

They left the embassy and J.T., Hope and Teagan regrouped with the guys, who were waiting for them at a small café.

Kirk, ever the ladies' man, was enjoying the view of Brazilian beauties who seemed to be everywhere.

"I think I've found my new ZIP code. Every woman is more beautiful than the last. Do they just grow them naturally gorgeous in this country?"

J.T. smiled at Kirk's humor, but his mind was too focused on the situation. Besides, as beautiful as all the women in Brazil were, none of them held a candle to Hope.

He didn't know when it'd happened to him, but Hope was all he wanted. If he didn't know better, he'd swear he'd caught dengue fever or something equally deadly because his brain wasn't operating on all four cylinders.

"So, what's the plan?" Harris asked, eager to get moving. "This place gives me a headache. Too much spice."

J.T. shared what Camille had told them. "We'll be hard-pressed to find anyone willing to go up against the guy. Apparently, he's something of a saint in many circles. But we found one person who isn't going to be singing his praises. Apparently, the guy's daughter disappeared and he believes Anso was responsible."

"Why would some rich guy risk everything by stealing a woman?" Harris asked. "Unless things work differently in this country, rich men don't usually have a problem finding women who want to be with them."

"Not all women," Hope reminded Harris with a sharp look, and immediately Harris apologized.

"Sorry, just blathering on like I do. No offense, Red."

Hope nodded her acceptance of his apology and J.T. continued, "And I don't know, but something tells me this guy has a God complex. He has enough money that he feels he can do whatever he wants and get away with it. And in a country like this, where corruption is fairly easy to fund, his arrogance is probably well earned."

"All right, let's find this guy and see what we can do," Ty said. "We're on a tight time frame. If anyone finds out that we're here sniffing around, we're going to have a helluva a time getting out of this country."

"And I have no interest in spending the rest of my life in a Brazilian prison," Harris quipped sourly. "The food alone will kill me."

"Mild salsa would kill that Irish gut of yours," Kirk teased, shoving Harris. "If it ain't bland potatoes and rubbery shoe leather, you complain about your poor tummy."

"Eat me," Harris shot back as they squeezed into a van to check out their only lead.

Anyone with a God complex was dangerous.

And a man with more money than most small countries? Deadly.

J.T. LISTENED TO the man tell his story, rage and an inborn need for justice filling his veins.

Ricardo García was a man burning with an impotent fire. J.T. could see the pain and anguish this father felt for the loss of his only daughter and he wished, not only for Hope's sake, but also for Ricardo's, that Anso died a slow, grisly death for his crimes.

"She was a good girl, always helpful to me after her mother died. She made the best *pão de queijo* in the world." Ricardo paused to wipe his eyes, the pain still very fresh. "She liked to buy fresh herbs at the market and that's when he saw her."

"Anso DeLeon?" J.T. supplied, and Ricardo nodded with a hard look.

"My Carina was beautiful, too beautiful, with a kind heart, I worried."

"What happened?"

"People said they saw DeLeon talking to her at the market. At first she found his attention flattering. She told me about him. I warned that rich men do not marry poor girls. We had nothing to offer a man such as he. I encouraged her to stay away from DeLeon. My gut said nothing but bad things could come of his attention. I did not trust that his intention was pure, and I was right. Witnesses say that my Carina was forcibly pushed into a car and she was never seen after that. I know it was DeLeon. I went to the police, but they were unhelpful, even hostile to my concerns. They said I was a stupid father to accuse a great man of trying to steal a girl when he could have any woman he chooses.

But I know he took my Carina. She would never leave me alone. She was a good girl."

"How old was your daughter when she disappeared?"

"Seventeen."

J.T. swore under his breath. In his military career he'd seen more than his share of misery in different countries as cultures clashed, but there was no mistaking this father's pain.

The sudden warmth of Hope's hand grasping his calmed his urge to break something.

Ricardo wiped at his eyes with a stoic gesture, his gaze hardening. "I will help you. But I will kill him if I get close enough. Don't stand in my way."

Teagan shared a look with J.T., then shrugged when Hope didn't offer any dissent. "That's your business."

They weren't there to be the ethics police and he was grateful Hope seemed to realize that. By the sound of it, Anso DeLeon didn't bother himself with ethics or morals, so it was probably time to pay for his karma earned, anyway.

"Do you have access to guns?" Ricardo asked point-blank.

Teagan nodded.

"Good. Then I have a way to get into the compound. I've been thinking of this plan for a year, but couldn't do it alone. If you have the guns, I have the plan."

"Sounds like a match made in heaven," Kirk said, grinning. "Let's do this. It's been too long since I smelled the sweet aroma of gunpowder in the morning."

"You crazy son of a bitch, you need your head checked," Harris growled, but he had that hungry look, too, and J.T. knew he had the best possible team for the job.

Even if they all went down in a hail of gunfire…at least he knew they'd take out a few of the bastards as they went down.

19

HOPE KNEW J.T. had lingering questions—conflicts, even— but she was too emotionally strung out to tackle them right now.

The trauma of the past forty-eight hours was something she didn't want to face, and J.T.'s arms seemed the safest place at the moment.

Especially when tonight was the night they were raiding Anso's compound.

They all had their pregame rituals, apparently.

J.T. had chosen to spend his with Hope.

She didn't want to read too much into his decision, but she was happy that he was there with her.

The option wasn't available, but if it were, Hope would walk away from this cursed place and forget she'd ever stepped foot on its soil.

Forget about the virus.

Forget about Anso.

Forget about what he planned to do with it.

But she couldn't do that.

Win or lose…it was all going down tonight.

Stop thinking.

Hope willed her brain to shut down, if only for this moment, these precious hours before go time.

"Kiss me, J.T.," she murmured as he tenderly helped her to the bed. His kisses were soft, almost reverent, and she sighed with pleasure as the sweetness of the stolen moment almost brought tears to her eyes.

They both knew the score—they were destined to crash and burn—but right now there was no denying that the thirst that raged between them was impossible to quench. They would have to ride it out to the bitter end, whatever that might be.

J.T. was her willing servant, kissing, touching, teasing, and yet he lost nothing in the manner of his masculinity as he worshipped her body. She thrilled at the sensual taking, the primal understanding that their bodies were meant to fit together in the most perfect way.

Hope simply drifted—no, plummeted—into utter pleasure, gasping as J.T. plundered her feminine folds, sinking between her thighs, marauding her core with that clever tongue until she was twisting and moaning, losing herself to the terrible sweetness of her climax.

Her chest heaved with the violence of her release as her entire body tingled and tensed as endorphins flooded her senses, blotting out every ache, every lingering fear. For a blissful moment, she was simply a vessel for extreme pleasure and she basked in the glow of that primal explosion.

"I'm addicted to you," J.T. admitted in a tight voice as he hungrily took her mouth, her own musk clinging to his lips, causing her to flush with fresh desire. "I don't think I'll ever get enough."

She knew that bittersweet feeling—that inescapable knowledge—and wrapped her arms around him tightly, begging him to sink into her, to impale her with his cock until they were one.

Hope gasped as the feeling of being filled, stretched

and taken started a new chain reaction of bliss. Her tightness clasped the turgid girth of his cock, milking him with loving abandon as they worked in tandem, giving to each other to accomplish one goal.

J.T.'s hips flexed as he thrust against her, going balls deep, shuddering with a groan as he withdrew, only to plunge deeper still. His broad shoulders braced him above her with perfect balance and Hope was struck by the sheer beauty of this incredible man.

He wasn't the kind of man you fell in love with, but Hope found her heart stirring. There was far more to J. T. Carmichael than he liked to let on. And it was that private person, the one who gave more than he took and risked his life for a near stranger in need, who was the person she was falling for.

Scared at the implication of such an admission, she clung to him even harder, afraid that she was making an even bigger mistake than creating the world's most dangerous virus.

But soon she could think of nothing more than the feel of J.T. buried inside her and she happily lost herself to the sensation of her inner core swelling with need as she tumbled into another release just as J.T. found his.

J.T. gasped, moaning her name as his wild thrusts slowly stopped, and he rolled to his back beside her. His chest rose and fell sharply as he tried to catch his breath, as overwhelmed as she by the explosive climax.

For a long moment, neither talked. Maybe they both were chewing on the same thought, the same worry, but neither was ready to tackle the conversation because they both knew the answer.

A tear snaked its way down her cheek and she wiped it away, her throat closing with emotion.

"I didn't think of the potential ramifications," she admitted in a small voice. Her statement could've applied to her work on the virus or the fact that she was falling in love with J.T. and she didn't clarify.

In answer, J.T. gathered her in his arms, but remained silent.

THEY MANAGED TO get the blueprints for the compound through a local Realtor who had connections to the contractor who'd built the house. It took greasing some palms, but they managed to make it worth his while to hand over the schematics.

Teagan and the crew had brought guns and were properly outfitted with enough of an arsenal to invade a small country. That was the upside to their collectively deadly military training—they knew how to handle themselves in a tight spot.

And wouldn't you know it, these crazy bastards actually missed getting shot at.

Kirk hefted his M16 and grinned, looking like a proud father. "Look at this baby. Isn't it a beauty? I call it the 'terrorist special'—able to mow down entire camps with one mag."

"I ain't gonna lie—it's a thing of beauty," Harris admitted, eyeing the assault rifle with envy. "But I'm a traditionalist. Nothing better than a good ole AK-47."

J.T. preferred the familiar comfort of his Glock. A bullet fired at high velocity, no matter where it was shot from, usually did the trick.

Ricardo had brought his own firepower and he had the look of a kamikaze pilot ready to go down with his plane. The grieving father didn't care if this was a one-way trip, but J.T. didn't want the guy to die. Ricardo was a good man and he deserved answers. God willing, he'd get some.

"Let's go over the plan one more time," Teagan said, all business. "Kirk and Harris will come with me and we'll take the south flank. Ricardo, J.T. and Ty will come around the north, clearing the way for Hope to get to the lab. This area here—" he pointed to the blueprints "—is the most vulnerable to entry. Chances are since your escape, there are probably dogs and more guards. Try to get in and out as quickly and quietly as possible. Do what you have to to stay alive, but try to limit the casualties. Let's remember, there might be civilians in this place being held against their will."

Ricardo reminded them, "Anso DeLeon is mine. If things don't go to plan, don't wait for me. I know the score. Whatever happens, just getting my chance to kill the bastard is enough reward. I've made peace with my god. You best do the same."

"My god encourages me to drink whiskey when I feel the need to confess something and then the feeling passes. Besides, the Almighty can be just as easily found in the bottle of whiskey as he can in a church," Harris said. "You ought to try it sometime."

"Leave the man to his beliefs. Just because you've renounced your faith, doesn't mean everyone else has," Ty said. "Let's hit it."

"I haven't renounced anything," Harris disagreed, grumbling as he climbed into the vehicle. "I'm on sabbatical."

They headed for the deep jungle, taking care to hide the vehicle before they set out on foot to the interior of the compound.

As expected, guards with dogs patrolled the perimeter, but as Teagan had pointed out, there was a place that was not patrolled due to the awkward angle at which the property edged into the dense jungle.

J.T. caught Hope's delicate shudder as no doubt bad memories surfaced. He squeezed her hand silently. No words were necessary.

There were no cameras and the fence was easy enough to scale.

They dropped soundlessly to the ground, except for Ricardo and Hope, whom they had to help up and over. J.T. hated bringing along civilians, as they were often a liability, but Hope wasn't going to stay behind and Ricardo had a score to settle.

The plan was to find a spot inside the perimeter and then wait until midnight to strike. They had the advantage of surprise on their side, but a sleeping household was a more easily contained target.

It was hard for J.T. to sit tight in his hiding spot patiently, but he knew from experience that rushing in half-cocked, juiced up on emotion, was the best way to get yourself shot.

On the last mission, not everyone from his squadron had returned.

Hell, sometimes he still heard Tommy Boy's rebel yell in his mind.

The kid had always been a hothead.

Now he was buried in Arkansas with full military honors, but J.T. was sure his family would much rather have their son back than the useless medal hanging on the wall.

Shaking off the bad memories, he focused on the task at hand.

Deep night fell, and with it, they moved stealthily through the compound, quietly dispatching guards as they went until they could breach the house.

THE WAITING HAD been the worst. Hope wasn't sure how the men had quietly sat like stone statues, waiting for the right time to strike. She'd been about to lose her mind.

Now, as she trailed behind J.T., his silent shadow, she wished she were sitting in the brush again.

It wasn't easy to watch J.T. kill a man, but she tried to remember that it was either the guards or one of them.

And Hope wasn't about to die tonight.

Hope followed J.T. as they headed for the lab, while the others went off in search of Anso, and they reached it without incident. She quickly punched in the code, and the door opened with a soft snick and they went inside.

She immediately went to the cold storage while J.T. covered the door.

She found her travel pack and the special container, but she didn't have time to don a containment suit, as would've been protocol if she weren't stealing the virus from a lunatic.

Hope took care to load the vials into the special container, lock it and jam it into her pack. Slinging the pack over her shoulder, they hightailed it out of the lab to the sound of erupting gunfire.

So much for a quiet in and out.

"I want you to hide," he told her even as she shook her head vehemently, but he insisted. "I have to make sure Teagan and the guys are okay. I will come back for you."

"No!" She gripped his arm. "Please don't go."

"I'm coming back. I just have to make sure that my brother gets out alive."

"I don't want to separate."

Hope could hear the panic in her voice, but she didn't care. She couldn't bear the thought of being left alone in this crazy place.

J.T. must've realized she was going to hold her ground and relented with a few choice swearwords, but she didn't care. They weren't separating. Not again.

He didn't look happy about it, but he didn't have time to argue. They followed the sound of gunfire, running across a dead guard here and there, but as luck would have it, four American men came running at full speed in their direction.

They didn't waste time on talk. As soon as J.T. saw them, he skidded to a stop and quickly changed direction, running back to the fence line. One by one they scaled the fence as if it were the easiest thing in the world and then J.T. hoisted Hope up and over with the assistance of his friends.

Within moments they were on the other side of the fence and Hope wasn't even sure how it had happened. The adrenaline rushing through her veins blotted out the fear of being shot. They put distance between themselves and the compound as they ran through the jungle until they found the car they'd stashed and squeezed into the older-model Blazer.

It wasn't until they were driving away that J.T. started talking again. "Where's Ricardo?" But judging by the tone of his voice, he already knew. "He didn't make it?"

"No," Teagan answered grimly.

"Please tell me one of you killed that son of a bitch DeLeon," she said, with an uncharacteristically vicious need for revenge. "That man didn't deserve to live another moment."

"Yeah, Ricardo got him."

"Well, at least he got what he deserved."

Before this adventure, Hope had always been more of a liberal, preferring incarceration over capital punishment. Not anymore.

Bad people needed to die.

But what about her? Was Anso right about her purposefully ignoring the true application of the virus she and Tanya had created?

The burden of that question weighed on her shoulders, but the answer scared her more.

Now more than ever, she had to get to the South American lab. "J.T., you have to take me to the lab. We have to get there before we leave this country."

"I take it our vacation adventure was just extended a little bit?" Kirk asked.

J.T. shared a look with Teagan and nodded grimly. "Gotta finish what we started."

Grateful, Hope closed her eyes and tried to calm her frantic heart. They would destroy the virus and everything would be all right.

It had to be.

20

KIRK AND HARRIS stayed behind while Teagan and Ty came with J.T. and Hope to the lab. Hope didn't protest the extra people, probably because she knew they were nonnegotiable.

The dirt road was filled with potholes and sections of washboard, which certainly would've deterred the hapless tourist who had gotten on the wrong road, but Hope assured them they were on the right path.

"I memorized the map before I left California. I knew if I ran into trouble, I'd need to know where I was going," she explained, adding with a slightly sheepish expression, "Another benefit of an eidetic memory."

"Damn." J.T. whistled, shaking his head. "I don't even want to know what your IQ is. I might never recover."

"Are you afraid of smart women?" she asked.

"Only ones I'm attracted to," he quipped, eliciting a blush on her part.

Teagan rolled his eyes. "Keep it in your pants, Romeo."

J.T. laughed and Hope averted her eyes, though a secret smile found her lips. God, she was sexy.

An hour on the road and Hope directed them to the gate,

giving Teagan the code to punch in. The gate swung open and they rolled through.

"No security?" Ty asked, finding that suspect. "Something doesn't feel right here."

"It's okay," Hope assured him. "That gate is electrified. It won't open without the right code and if anyone tries to scale it, they'll fry. So, yeah, don't touch the fence."

"Good to know."

They went deeper into the complex and parked in the near-empty parking lot.

"Boy, when you say it's an ultrasecret lab, you aren't joking. The employee picnic must be a real snore," Teagan said, glancing around. "Are you sure this lab is operational?"

Hope seemed to share his concern. "There should be more employees. C'mon, the entrance is over here."

She produced a key card from her bag and the door popped open with a soft click.

"The virus storage is on the top level, same as the lab in California," Hope explained, taking the lead, but J.T. had a weird tingle at the base of his skull that didn't bode well.

He pulled his gun for good measure, and Teagan and Ty did the same.

They took the stairs because J.T. didn't trust the elevator. There was power running through the small complex, but it was a ghost town and that was beyond strange.

Hope slid her key card into the lock and the door opened, but was stopped by something on the other side of the door.

J.T. halted Hope before she could push the door open and directed her behind him. Teagan and Ty flanked him for backup as J.T. pushed against the resistance to open the door.

Hearing nothing but dead silence, J.T. entered the room to find what was causing the resistance.

A body.

Hope stuffed back a scream as she stared at the man in a lab coat sprawled out with dried blood staining the floor.

"Oh, my God!" she gasped, edging away from the blood spill. Then she saw that the dead scientist hadn't been alone. There were two other bodies, another man and a woman, slumped over their stations, staring sightless at the walls. "What happened here?"

"Something bad," Ty replied darkly. "I say we get the hell out of here before whoever did this comes back."

"I don't understand... Anso is dead. Who would do this?" Hope asked, panicked. She scanned the room for answers, her gaze desperate. She looked to J.T. "I have to tell Deirdre. There must be some kind of protocol. This room is supposed to be a clean room. There could be contamination." Suddenly, she lost the panic and hustled to another section of the room.

J.T. went after her. "What is it?"

She opened a closet and pulled out a huge white suit and climbed into it. "I have to make sure that the samples that are housed here haven't been compromised. Stay here."

"Think again," J.T. said in a low tone. "You don't know what happened to these people and if there's some dangerous viruses turned loose in that room, you're not going in."

Hope ignored him and zipped the suit. "I'm the only person qualified to go in there. The suit will keep me safe. I have to know."

Teagan stopped J.T. "She's right. Let her go. She's the only one who can."

He didn't care what'd happened here. Dead scientists, dangerous viruses—he wanted to put this place in his rearview mirror, but he knew Hope wasn't going to leave until she knew there hadn't been a breach. "Fine. You've got two minutes and then we're getting the hell out of here."

Hope pulled the protective cover over her head and walked into the cold storage where the viruses were held.

"I don't like this," J.T. growled to Teagan.

Ty went to a computer and started nosing around, but came up empty. "Nothing here. Whoever was here didn't much care about what was on the computers."

Hope reappeared and pulled her cover free. "Someone destroyed the samples. There's nothing left."

An idea came to J.T., one that was borderline crazy, but considering their options seemed almost brilliant.

"Destroy your samples, too. It'll look like whoever broke in was responsible for everything," J.T. said, shocking Hope. "It's the best way to come out smelling like a rose in this deal. Otherwise, you'll always worry that someone out there is abusing the virus."

Even though the plan had been to destroy the samples, Hope suddenly hesitated, turning to him almost desperately. "This is my life's work," she said, torn. "I mean, not only mine, but Tanya's, too. And it doesn't belong to me. It belongs to Tessara. Maybe it's not right to destroy it."

"No one needs that kind of power," J.T. said in a low tone. "Especially a company like Tessara."

Teagan urged them to make a decision. "Time's short, man. Shit or get off the pot—we gotta blow this place."

J.T. met Hope's gaze. *Please destroy it.* Everything hinged on that one decision.

Hope's mouth firmed as she nodded slowly.

"You're right. This is what needs to happen." She grabbed her pack, pulled her protective hood back on and disappeared into the cold-storage room.

21

THE COLD-STORAGE door closed firmly behind her, sealing the room. While the room was used to store the live viruses, it was also equipped with the machinery to destroy them.

As she approached the machine, vials in hand, Hope's resolve wobbled again.

Am I doing the right thing?

She wasn't usually this indecisive, but then she'd never been faced with such a potentially big consequence in her hands.

It wasn't only her life's work on the line; Tanya had died for this breakthrough and even though there were potential ramifications if it were to fall in the wrong hands, the potential good it could do was astounding.

Was she being selfish? She didn't like to think so, but she hated to think that Tanya had died for nothing.

J.T. didn't agree with her decision to go back to Tessara and talk to Deirdre, but she had to get a feel for what was going on in their lab. What if Deirdre wasn't the mole and she was as clueless as the rest of them about who was secretly monitoring their projects? Didn't she owe it to Tessara to give them the chance to prove themselves before she destroyed company property?

Of course, the small print was that she would probably lose her job and likely face prison if it was found out that she'd destroyed the samples without permission, but that was a small price to pay for doing the right thing.

Hope worried her bottom lip. Wasn't it?

Okay, so the truth was she didn't want to go to jail. Starchy foods didn't agree with her digestion and orange was not her color.

But she wasn't a spy or trained to know if someone was lying, so how would she know if Deirdre was some kind of criminal mastermind or simply a power-hungry supervisor with zero sense of humor?

She could picture the watercooler chatter.

"Oh, how was South America? What did you do?"

"Great! I stole company property, crash-landed in Mexico, slept in the jungle, rode in the back of an old pickup truck to a small airport, only to fly to South America and be kidnapped by a crazy sociopathic billionaire who planned to beat me with a whip when I didn't agree to weaponize the virus I created. Oh, and I had some great local cuisine while I was there!" Pause. "What did I miss while I was gone?"

But as Hope knew, if anyone actually asked about her vacation, she would make up some grand lie about a boring staycation that involved binge-watching *Downton Abbey* and eating ice cream straight from the carton.

She pulled the vials carefully from the container, resigned to destroying them. J.T. was right—they were simply too dangerous to leave to chance.

She slid the vials into the autoclave machine, snapped the door shut and locked it, then pushed the button to eradicate the only viable samples of the virus on the planet.

A mixture of sadness and relief flooded her as she

watched the timer. There was no turning back now. She and Tanya had already doctored their notes to show that their attempts had ended in failure. The only proof that they'd been successful was being cooked at 121 degrees Fahrenheit and the formula was locked inside Hope's head, where it would remain for the rest of her life.

"I hope I made the right decision," she murmured with a quick prayer, and then exited the lab. Once clear, she removed her biohazard suit and tossed it down the chute for the incinerator and returned to the room where she'd left the guys.

"It's done," she said, drawing a deep breath. "It'll take an hour for the process, but the vials are unmarked. No one will know what was in them. They'll just assume that someone was following protocol for live toxins when all hell broke loose here."

"Works for me," Teagan said, still on edge. "I say we blow this place now before whoever did this decides to come back."

"I need to do one last thing," she said, going to a panel and opening it.

"What are you doing?" J.T. asked, wary.

"I used my key card to get in here, which is an electronic record. I have to call it in or else I won't be able to answer questions without raising suspicion. Tanya had already prearranged for my trip here, so if I don't make it look as if I was just following instructions, they will look deeper."

"Good point," J.T. agreed, motioning. "Go ahead."

Hope swallowed and made the call straight to Deirdre with the appropriate amount of terror in her voice.

"Something terrible happened here," she told Deirdre, waking her with the news. It was the middle of the night in California. "I don't know what to do!"

Deirdre, a no-nonsense type A personality, snapped into efficiency mode. "Are you safe?"

"I think so. Whoever did this was gone by the time I arrived."

"Good. I will alert the authorities. I want you to leave. We will take care of the details."

Hope was happy to be off the hook and gratefully agreed. Deirdre clicked off and Hope turned to the guys and said, "Let's get the hell out of here before she changes her mind," and they bailed.

THE FOLLOWING MORNING J.T. awoke to a spicy aroma that was welcome to his growling belly.

Hope smiled, already dressed. "There was a street vendor outside the hotel. It smells pretty good. The guys already ate theirs, so I'm guessing it's safe. No threat of food poisoning."

Swinging his legs over the bed, he tugged on his jeans. Hope looked like a vision out of his most erotic dreams, her hair pulled into a messy bun at the top of her head, her glasses perched on her cute nose, dressed in a soft short white linen dress that clung to her curves and made him want to rip it off.

"What's on the menu, aside from you?" he asked with a playful growl, tugging her close to nuzzle her neck. "Smells incredible."

"Me or the breakfast?"

"Both."

She laughed and pulled away. "It's nothing fancy, chorizo and eggs in a tortilla."

"Sounds like my kind of breakfast."

Hope laughed and handed him his burrito, but even as she smiled, there was something else behind her eyes that made him pause.

"Are you okay?"

"Great!" she returned brightly, but she was nervous. "Is it good?"

"Delicious," he answered around a hot bite, still trying to decipher her strange behavior. "Are you sure nothing is bothering you? You seem on edge."

"Actually, yes, there is something we should talk about," she started, and he had a feeling he knew where this was going because he'd been grappling with it, too.

There was something happening between them that felt a lot deeper than simply lust.

The other night had felt different.

It hadn't been just sex.

It hadn't been two people fulfilling a need, scratching an itch.

The sex had felt more like...making love.

He didn't believe in love at first sight—lust, sure. But falling head over heels in love with a virtual stranger was a fairy tale and he was much too old to believe in nonsense made for kids.

But if that were true, how was it that he wasn't nailing down the details of his promised payment?

The fact that he couldn't give a shit about the money was telling.

Fall in love with a brainiac like Hope? Sure. That made sense.

They had zero in common.

Aside from the insane chemistry between the sheets, but what about real-life stuff?

How did she feel about gun control? He owned an arsenal.

How did she feel about global warming? He couldn't give a shit.

How did she feel about mustard or mayo on her sandwich? Mustard was appropriate for all sandwiches, at all times. Mayo was disgusting.

And more important, how the hell had she not considered the potential danger of her research if it fell into the wrong hands? Why hadn't she cared?

But even as the questions lingered, he wasn't ready to tackle them yet, so he deliberately switched tracks.

"So, what's the plan now?"

Hope seemed relieved to talk about something other than what was sitting between them.

"Deirdre called me early this morning while you were still sleeping. Tessara hates bad press. They handled the situation quickly and quietly. Deirdre said the violence was due to local militia trying to get their hands on chemicals they could manufacture drugs with, which is why nothing was missing that truly could've been disastrous."

"Dumb criminals, zero. Tessara, one."

"Yeah, except for the scientists who were killed. I'd say they lost that round."

"True enough."

"But the good news is that no one suspects anything about why I was really there. I still have my job and I'm not going to face jail time. I call that a win-win," she said with a heavy sigh that belied the sentiment. He understood her feelings on that score. It was hard to fully appreciate a victory when it came at such a heavy cost.

J.T. finished his burrito. "I'm glad," he said, and he meant it. He didn't want Hope getting in trouble when she'd worked so hard to make it right, but he was anxious to know what happened next, even if the answer scared him. "Where does that leave us?"

She paused, her gaze darting. "Us? You mean…?"

Here was his opportunity to jump in with both feet, but because she didn't take point, he chickened out. "No, I mean about our business relationship. I'm still out one plane," he reminded her, cursing himself for being a pussy.

"Oh! Of course," Hope said, flustered. "Yes, Tessara will pay my expenses. I will explain to Deirdre what happened and she'll have Accounting cut a check. That shouldn't be a problem, especially when they want to keep this incident quiet."

"Are you actually going to keep working for that company?" he asked, incredulous, channeling his frustration into something else. "I mean, c'mon, don't you think you might want to start shopping your résumé around?"

"Tessara does good work," she protested stiffly. "The innovations that come out of our labs are second to none. What if Tessara discovers a cure for cancer? Why wouldn't I want to be a part of that?"

"And what if they discover a way to turn people into half monkeys in some weird, unsanctioned, highly illegal experiment gone wrong? Tessara is dangerous."

"One, that's ridiculous, and two, I think that's not your concern. I will pay for your plane and the agreed-upon fee. Tessara will pay for my return flight. You and your brother can return on your own, if you choose."

"So that's it? 'Sayonara, babe—it's been real'?"

"Not exactly, but you're pushing it that way by maligning the company I work for."

"I call 'em as I see 'em."

"As do I. Your opinion was not asked for or appreciated."

Well, that was just great. "This is the thanks I get for risking my neck. Have you forgotten that it was Tessara that put you in this mess?"

"It wasn't Tessara," she returned hotly. "It was Anso DeLeon."

"Yeah? And who told DeLeon about your project? There's still a missing link and you're naive if you think it wasn't an inside job, which also means that you're still not safe with Tessara."

That was pretty solid logic, but in his experience women

rarely listened to logic when they were heated, and Hope was no exception, in spite of her brainpower.

"I appreciate everything you've done. I will make sure you are compensated generously for your services. I've called a cab. I just wanted to—" she hesitated, swallowing "—say goodbye properly."

Properly? "Thanks," he said. "Real considerate of you. Is the burrito my tip for saving your ass repeatedly?"

She blinked back sudden tears. "Why are you making this so difficult? I was trying to be nice. I thought you might be hungry."

"And I was hungry, but I didn't expect you to feed me bullshit alongside my chorizo."

"It's not bullshit."

"It is." He rose and stalked to her, crowding her space. He cupped her face, angry, but hurt, too. "It's all bullshit to cover up what you don't really want to talk about."

"You're wrong," she tried saying, but J.T. was done with listening and sealed his mouth to hers, drinking in the taste of her, savoring the feel of her soft lips against his.

She groaned into his mouth as their tongues tangled. The heat between them intensified. Even pissed as hell, he wanted her. He pulled her close, his hands roaming her backside.

Within seconds he was erect and ready. As he pressed himself against her, she moaned in response, melting against him.

"I was hoping breakfast might soften the blow," she gasped, as he lifted her dress and found her damp and hot core.

"The burrito wasn't *that* good," he growled, pinning her against the wall. His questing fingers pushed aside her panties to find her dewy folds. "Is this where you say, 'It's not you—it's me'? Honey, I invented that speech."

"J.T., I appreciate everything you've done for me and I know I owe you a plane—"

"Screw the plane," he cut in, pushing his finger inside her willing heat as she shuddered at the sensual invasion. Was she breaking up with him? Well, technically they weren't dating, so they couldn't break up, but it felt the same when she was giving him the heave-ho.

And he wasn't ready to let her go.

"You and I both know that this was a short-term thing." She caught her breath on a groan, then continued in a breathy tone. "I think it's best if we both admit that we know it's not going to last and we ought to cut our losses now before things get messy."

"I'd say things are already messy." He removed his finger and sucked her juices off with a hungry grin.

She blushed a pretty shade of pink. "That's not what I mean."

"I know what you meant. Yeah, sure. I get where you're coming from. I mean, you and me just doesn't make sense in the big picture. There's only so much sex a person can have, right?"

At the mention of their sexual chemistry, she inhaled a sharp breath and he secretly enjoyed that he had that effect on her. Sucked to be the only one with a dog in the fight.

But even as she was trying to bail on him, her fingers were impatiently plucking at his buttons and he didn't mind. Especially when her hot little hand circled around his cock, squeezing him tight.

"We shouldn't…" she tried saying as he hoisted her on his lap, holding her against the wall.

"Yeah, tell me about it," he agreed, but all he could focus on was that sweet spot between her thighs and how much he wanted to pin her to the wall with his cock.

He shoved himself deep inside her and she shuddered as she clung to him, her legs wrapped tightly around him.

"Oh, God, J.T.," she moaned loudly, impaled on his length. He held her firmly as he thrust against her, loving the sound of her gasps and tiny cries of pleasure.

There was something so primal about taking her like this that he had little control over how quickly his body began to prime for his release.

With an animalistic grunt he poured into her, losing himself as he came. He dimly heard her cry out his name as she climaxed, too.

For a long moment he remained buried inside her and she clung to him, anchoring him in place. Their breathing harsh, their heartbeats one.

Slowly, he let her down and she fell to the bed while he tucked himself away and buttoned his jeans. Her hair was tousled and she looked deliciously screwed, and he had to remind himself to start thinking straight—with his head, not his dick.

She'd been giving him the boot.

He sat beside her with a sigh and she struggled to sit up, modestly fixing her dress with a chagrined smile.

"That seems to happen a lot between us," she said with half a laugh.

True enough. But intense heat notwithstanding, he knew she was right. They didn't have a future together and he should've been relieved that she'd come to that realization on her own. So why was he suffering with the very real sensation of being rejected?

"What's really the deal?" he asked point-blank.

"What do you mean?"

"C'mon, we both know that something else is eating at you—just come out and say it. Don't you think we've been through enough to at least be honest with each other?"

"I am trying to be honest," she insisted with a distressed frown. "Don't you see that it's better this way?"

"Sure, on the surface I would agree with you. But have

you forgotten that you're not exactly safe just yet? If you think I risked my ass to save yours just to have you get killed Stateside, you're crazy."

Hope stiffened. "I can take care of myself."

"That didn't come out right. What I mean is, I don't want anything to happen to you and I'm not saying we have to put labels on things, but I care about you and I'm not about to let anything happen to you."

The fire went out of Hope's eyes and she actually risked a small smile. "I know you care about me," she said, her tone warming. "I care about you, too. I'm trying to lessen the hurt when whatever this is…ends."

"Let's cross that bridge when we come to it. In the meantime, I say we find the son of a bitch who was truly behind all this so we can safely put this situation to bed without worrying that someone is still out there looking to kidnap or kill you, because you know those are the only options."

Hope, aghast, said, "And why are those the only options?"

"Because if you're not working for them, you're working against them and that's a risk they won't take."

She couldn't argue with his logic and nodded. "I guess you're right. I'm still in shock that any of this happened. Three weeks ago I was consumed with the biggest scientific breakthrough of the century… Now I'm looking behind my back for killers and sociopaths."

"Have you considered going into a less dangerous line of work? I've heard there's an opening on the bomb squad," he offered, only half joking.

"Ha-ha."

He knew he shouldn't, but he couldn't quite resist. Pulling her into his arms, he ignored her halfhearted protest and kissed her long and deep. She melted against him, fitting against his body as if they were molded for each another, but she soon pulled away and stood when a horn sounded outside.

"That's my cab. I have to go."

"Wait… Come back with us," he suggested, not ready to watch her leave.

"I can't. I have to get back to work if I'm going to pull this off. There's no reason I would return with you and my supervisor would question it."

"Is that the only reason you're returning on Tessara's dime?"

She didn't answer. "I'll connect with you back in California. Thank you, J.T. For everything."

He didn't want her thanks—he wanted her.

22

THE FLIGHT HOME was uneventful. With J.T. broody and in a foul mood, the guys gave him a wide berth until they landed and were unloading the plane.

He knew he needed to snap out of it. His buddies had done something so selfless for him that words couldn't convey how appreciative he truly was, and he hoped they knew that, in spite of his surly attitude.

The best part about that group was that words weren't needed.

Kirk slapped J.T. on the back with a grin. "She's hot."

"No argument there," he said, not bothering to hide anything.

Kirk, Ty and Harris filed into the house while Teagan hung back.

"You all right, man?"

"Worn-out," J.T. answered, which was the truth, but it wasn't only physical fatigue pulling at him. The entire ride home all he could think was how easily Hope had been able to walk away. It sucked to be the one being left. Usually he was the one making tracks, not the other way around. "Thanks for saving my ass. Again."

"What are brothers for?"

"Yeah, but something tells me most guys don't have to fly to other countries to bail out their brothers."

"True. I might look forward to a phone call where you're just asking to borrow money." He playfully punched J.T. in the arm. "Seriously, though, what the hell happened?"

"As soon as I figure it out, you'll be the first to know."

"I hope she's worth it."

"It's not like we're dating or anything. I'll get over it."

Teagan saw through his bluff. "You can tell yourself whatever you want, but the truth is…you have feelings for her. You wouldn't have done all this for just some client."

"A client working for a company with deep pockets," he reminded his brother. "You'll thank me later when that check arrives."

"Speaking of, we need to talk about Blue Yonder," Teagan said, then added with a wave, "Later."

Yeah, funny thing, now that they would have the money to keep the charter going, he didn't care.

He'd been hell-bent to keep the charter going only a week ago. Now? He could see how the charter was foundering. He'd selfishly wanted to hold on to it when his brother had been trying to tell him it was time to cut their losses.

Maybe he didn't need Blue Yonder any longer.

Blue Yonder had been Teagan's solution to J.T.'s unraveling after his time in the service. He'd been through the ringer during his last tour.

The memories had nearly eaten him alive.

Blue Yonder had given him something else to pour his focus into.

The charter's failure hadn't been something he could handle.

Now he saw it for what it was—a money pit.

And his brother would stick with him no matter what,

even if he went down in flames trying to save it because that was what J.T. wanted.

Why hadn't he seen what an ass he was being?

It still stung to think of letting Blue Yonder go, but after everything that'd happened, it didn't seem as important to hold on to it.

He was tired as hell, but he needed to think, and he wouldn't be able to do that with Kirk and the rest of the guys at the house. They were good guys—but loud. When Harris started in on the whiskey, no one would be sleeping tonight.

Climbing into his truck, he realized the one place he wanted to go was the one place he wasn't invited.

Not to mention he hadn't a clue where Hope lived.

Suddenly, his cell phone chirped and he saw a text message from Teagan.

From Ty: 3212 Sutton Avenue, apt. 27. You're welcome.

He grinned. "Bless your hacking little soul," he murmured, returning his cell to his pocket. There were benefits to having friends who were smarter with computers than you were.

But even though he had her address and the urge to follow up was stronger than he wanted to admit…he held back.

What was he? Some kind of stalker? How would he feel if some woman he'd cut ties with suddenly showed up on his doorstep?

It would be uncomfortable as hell.

So there was his answer.

Don't go there.

At least not tonight.

Give it some time to breathe.

Maybe he'd feel different in a few days' time.

Hell, maybe whatever this was—this heart-pounding, desperate need to feel her in his arms—would fade and he could go back to feeling normal again.

Yeah. Maybe.

Or maybe it would get worse.

In the meantime, his affliction was nothing that a strong whiskey couldn't fix.

Sweet oblivion, here I come.

HOPE SLID INTO the bath, sighing as the hot water soothed her troubled heart.

Leaving J.T. had been the most difficult thing she'd had to do, but she wasn't about to encourage something that she knew had no future.

J.T. was a player, a man who liked to live a cavalier life. She was excruciatingly type A, a woman who liked to have all details planned out before she embarked on a task or project.

And that included the relationships in her life.

Although nothing had gone to plan from the moment she'd stepped onto Blue Yonder's stretch of tarmac.

Everything had gone to hell in a handbasket, but J.T. had managed to navigate every obstacle with a grace that was almost superhuman.

They didn't make many men like J.T. and his band of brothers anymore.

And the way that man could make her shudder and moan with a touch… Ugh. How was she ever going to forget that heat?

No man would ever measure up to J. T. Carmichael in the sex department. The man had been…extremely talented.

She should've given J.T. her address. But then he would've shown up and where would that have taken them?

Her heart rate leaped at the idea of seeing J.T. at her door.

Wishful imaginings were harmful in the long run, she chastised herself when she lingered a little too long on that fantasy.

Nothing had changed. They were still incompatible in the big scheme of things and that wasn't likely to change. She wasn't about to embark on an ill-fated relationship that was doomed from the start.

She'd have to be a complete idiot to do that.

Hope was alive thanks to J.T.—she couldn't forget that part.

Had she hurt him by walking away? Hope liked to think that she hadn't crushed him, but in her heart, she knew she'd caused terrible pain.

How did she know that? Because she'd felt it, too.

Each step away from the hotel had been agony. Climbing into the cab as if nothing had happened was like swallowing razors.

And each night since, she'd been tormented by dreams that'd left her aching and reaching for someone who wasn't there.

Her bed had never been so lonely until now. There was definitely a J.T.-sized deficit in her life right now and she alternated between being irritated at her weepiness and intensely depressed over how weepy she was.

Tomorrow she had a meeting with Deirdre to discuss the details as she knew them—edited, of course—about the South American incident. It was a formality, but a necessary one to satisfy the authorities and clear Tessara of any responsibility.

The report was also necessary for the insurance company to release funds for the damages done to the lab and any payout to the families that might be required.

It was all very tidy.

That should've appealed to her.

The fact that there were very few loose ends to tie up should've made her sigh with relief, but instead she was troubled by how neat it was.

Shouldn't there be more paperwork? More questions?

Just like when Tanya was killed.

Business as usual. Life goes on.

But Tanya had been more than her supervisor; she'd been her friend.

"There's a rumor out there that there's more to life than science," Tanya had teased over Chinese food in the break room late one night. "I'm thinking of signing up for one of those online dating sites and testing out that theory."

"You could end up with a serial killer."

"That fear is so 1990s. Everyone knows that the professional sect doesn't have time to socialize in the traditional ways, so places like eSoulmate.com fill the gap. I like that it separates people into two categories, those most likely to be looking for a fun, but ultimately short-lived relationship and those who are marriage material."

"Oh?" Hope raised an eyebrow as she slurped down her chow mein. "So what exactly are you looking for? A hot sweaty time or matrimony?"

"Well, to run the risk of sounding like a pathetic sap, I'd love to find someone who I can get hot and sweaty with and still end up with a ring on my finger. Maybe a hot physicist or something."

"Are physicists hot?" Hope asked dubiously. "Have you seen the physicists walking the halls at Tessara? Definitely not hot."

"True. But I find intelligence very sexy. However, I also find burly men in kilts sexy. Do you think I can find those attributes in one man?"

Hope laughed. "Good luck. Can you imagine Wesley in a kilt?"

"Wesley Gibson? God, no. Nobody wants to see that."

"There's your answer. I think you have to take one over the other."

"In that case, I'll take a torrid affair with a hot, intellectually inferior guy and then when I'm finished with him— or rather my vagina screams for mercy—I'll start looking around for the guy who will father my children and fantasize about the man who used to bend me in a pretzel."

At that Hope broke into peals of laughter and nearly choked on a soggy noodle.

"Good luck," she managed, and they both dissolved into giggles like teenagers.

Hope broke out of her reverie and realized her water was cold.

"I miss you, Tanya," she murmured as she climbed from the tub and released the plug to drain it. "I hope heaven is overrun with sexy, smart guys with great burly thighs just for you, my friend."

Hope wiped at the sudden tears and tucked her robe around her.

She'd never admit it out loud, but she missed J.T. more than she should.

J.T. had been her smart, sexy—no, incredibly sexy— adventure and she hadn't been ready to give him up.

Sighing heavily, she climbed into bed and tried to find sleep.

J.T. had planted questions in her head—questions without easy answers.

Was there a mole embedded within Tessara? And if so, did that mean she was still in danger?

More than ever she wished J.T. were beside her.

But that wasn't logical.

Nothing about their relationship had been logical.

Maybe that'd been the best part.

23

HOPE STEPPED OFF onto the level-four lab and was surprised to find Deirdre flipping through her notes. It was hard not to react by ripping them out of Deirdre's bony fingers, but somehow she managed a false smile.

"Good morning," she said, wondering why Deirdre would be using her notebook for light reading. Deirdre had access to her finalized findings, which were submitted each week, but her scribblings were her own. "Anything I can help you find?"

Snapping the notebook closed, she gestured, saying, "Follow me, Dr. Larsen," and walked at a brisk clip from the lab into the offices.

Tanya's office, still closed since her death, made Hope swallow the immediate lump that bobbed in her throat. She knew Deirdre was interviewing Tanya's replacement, but for Hope no one would measure up to her friend.

Deirdre didn't seem affected in the least by Hope's grief and wasn't sympathetic, either.

In fact, they'd been business as usual the day after Tanya had died.

Going straight to the point, Deirdre said, "Tell me about

the project you and Dr. Fields were working on when she died."

Hope paused, arranging her answer in her head. "We were working on the C1H4 protocol, but we were unable to crack the gene sequencing."

"None of the samples were viable?" Deirdre asked, even though Hope knew her notes supported that assumption.

"No, ma'am."

"So why the trip to the South American lab?"

"Dr. Fields wanted me to acquire the Ebola sample so we could cross-reference our findings against the parent virus."

"And a courier service couldn't have accomplished this?"

"She didn't trust the courier. Plus, to be honest, I'd admitted that I'd never been to South America and it was on my bucket list. She said if I could combine business and pleasure, I could pick up the sample for her."

"Interesting."

"Interesting? How so? Was this outside of company policy?"

Instead of answering, Deirdre asked another question. "Your expense request is quite large. Care to explain?"

"Unbeknownst to me, someone had been following me. Perhaps the same people who broke into the South American lab. They shot at the plane I was on and it crash-landed in Mexico. I managed to get to the South American lab only because of Mr. Carmichael's help. Is there a problem with the expense request?"

Deirdre waved away the question. "That's not the problem. Just trying to solve a small mystery. It seems odd to me that someone was chasing after you. Why? The attack on the Brazilian lab was due to gang violence. What possible cause would someone have to shoot down your plane?

Pardon my rudeness, but I didn't realize you and Tanya were working on anything of importance."

This was it. Deirdre had realized that she and Tanya had doctored the books. The plan had been to contain the samples at the South American lab, but to list the samples as nonviable, and thus what would be destroyed was simply biological waste.

But if Deirdre knew that Tanya and Hope were lying, which side was Deirdre on?

She heard J.T.'s voice in her head, warning about the possible mole in Tessara, and she held back the urge to tell Deirdre the plain truth.

"I have no idea, but it was very frightening," Hope said, holding Deirdre's gaze without flinching. She was a terrible poker player, but she knew it was important to convince Deirdre that she was telling the truth.

"Yes, I can only imagine. You must've been relieved to take a commercial flight home."

"Very much so. I've had my fill of charter planes."

"As would I." Deirdre grabbed a piece of paper and signed off on the expense request, then slid it over to Hope. "Your expenses have been approved."

Hope smiled and rose. "Thank you." Assuming Deirdre was finished, she turned to leave, but Deirdre's voice at her back stopped her dead.

"Do you know of Anso DeLeon?"

Hope swallowed and turned, affecting an expression of vague recollection. "The name sounds familiar, but I can't quite place it."

"Mr. DeLeon is a patron of the sciences. A philanthropist who has donated millions to Tessara for research projects. It's thanks to his generous contribution that your lab project was funded at all."

"Oh? What a nice man." She nearly choked on the words. "Forgive me—why do you ask?"

Deirdre steepled her fingers. "He was killed three days ago. Home invasion in his South American home. Isn't that a strange coincidence, that he was killed during the same time frame as your visit to Brazil?"

"Very."

"Hmm…the world has lost a great man."

Hardly. The world was a better place with him gone. "Sounds like it." Sweat began to gather at Hope's temple. "Was there anything else you needed?"

"No, I think you've answered my questions sufficiently."

Hope forced a smile. "Great. I'll head back to the lab."

"Yes, I would like you to continue the work on C1H4. Your notes seem promising."

"Of course," Hope answered, wondering how long she could sabotage her own work before Deirdre caught on. J.T. was right—maybe she ought to start shopping her résumé after all.

Hope hustled down the hall, her brain whirring faster than a centrifuge. Everything about that meeting had set her hair on end. Was Deirdre corrupt? Was Tessara as bad as J.T. thought it was? Good people worked for Tessara; she knew that because Tanya had been one of the best.

She slipped into the restroom, needing a minute to calm her beating heart. The walls were closing in. Tessara didn't feel safe any longer. More than anything, she wished J.T. were around to protect her. Under most circumstances she was very "I am woman, hear me roar", but her South American experience had taught her the value of a big, strong man with a bigger gun having her back.

The fact that Deirdre even brought up DeLeon's name made her break out into a cold sweat. Was Deirdre in DeLeon's pocket? She would've had access to Tanya and Hope's research.

A sick, queasy feeling sat lodged in her gut, twisting the bagel she'd eaten for breakfast.

As she stared at her reflection in the mirror, she realized she felt more trapped now than when she'd been hurtling to the ground in a rapidly descending plane.

What was she going to do?

She didn't know who to trust or where to turn.

To quote Tanya…she was in quite a pickle.

J.T. RECEIVED TESSARA'S check in the mail and immediately handed it over to Teagan, but he felt no sense of satisfaction at seeing all those zeros.

"Nice to be in the black again," Teagan said. When he saw J.T.'s expression hadn't changed, he added, "It's been a week since we got back and you've had her address. Why haven't you gone to see her?"

"What's the point? I'm not that guy who chases after women who've given him the brush-off. There are plenty of fish in the sea—isn't that how the saying goes?"

"Yeah, well, this one was different."

He scowled. "What makes you say that?"

"Because it's been a week and you're getting worse each day. Yesterday you just about bit my head off when I asked you if there was any more beer in the fridge."

It was true. He'd been thinking about Hope, and the fact that he was still thinking about her when he should've moved on was putting him in a foul mood.

The worst.

"Just go talk to her. Maybe things look different now."

"Why would they look different? She doesn't want to be with me. She was pretty plain about her meaning. She's a brainiac, and I'm just a pilot."

"An ex-fighter pilot in the Air Force, Special Forces—don't forget that part," Teagan replied, clearly amused at how bristly J.T. was being. "Is this what love looks like? If so, I think I'll pass."

"I'm not in love," J.T. shot back, but just the thought of Hope made his heart ache. "I think I'm coming down with something."

"Yeah, it's called Cupiditis."

He skewered Teagan with a dark look when Teagan laughed at his own joke.

"Okay, all kidding aside, your pride is keeping you from going to her, not some belief that she doesn't want you. You want her to come to you—that way you're the one in control because that's the way you operate."

"That's utter bullshit."

"Oh, c'mon, you know I'm right. What would happen if she showed up right now? Would you tell her to hit the bricks or would you pull her into the bedroom and make things awkward for the rest of us?"

He had to grin. Their hotel sex had been pretty vigorous and the walls had been thin. J.T. didn't need to insult Teagan by lying; they both knew the score. "She doesn't want me," he said mulishly. "That's her loss."

"I'm no expert on love, but I saw the way she looked at you. What if she pushed you away to protect herself? Maybe she's just as gun-shy about love as you are."

J.T. opened his mouth to shoot his brother down, but there was something that rang true. What if that were the case and they were both doing the same thing?

"Just go see her. Figure things out. Stop being afraid and see where it takes you."

"What if takes me straight to the bottom? I really don't feel like being kicked to the curb twice."

"I'm not going to lie—it could happen, but what if it doesn't? What if she's happy to see you? Wouldn't that be worth the risk?"

He considered the possibility and the fact that his heart tripled in beat at the idea told him what he needed to know.

"Am I being a giant pussy?"

"The fact that you have to ask means you already know the answer."

"Asshole. You could've lied."

Teagan laughed and clapped him on the shoulder. "Stop your bellyaching and go get your woman."

His woman.

He liked the sound of that.

Hopefully, Hope did, too.

Otherwise, his heart was about to take another beating of epic proportion.

24

MAYBE SHE WAS paranoid, but every shadow seemed menacing and every sound was like a harbinger of potential danger. Had Tanya been aware that her days were numbered or had she gone about her day, popping into Subway for a sandwich, only to die moments later with a turkey on sourdough in her hand?

Hope felt as if the Grim Reaper were counting out the sands in her hourglass, which was ridiculous because she didn't believe in stuff like that, but her brain was playing tricks on her.

Last night she could've sworn she'd heard someone in her living room, but when she'd gotten up to investigate—holding a baseball bat for protection—there'd been nothing out of place and no one lurking to murder her.

It was official: she was totally paranoid.

Even at Tessara it felt as if eyes were on her. When before she'd blithely walked the halls, her mind occupied with formulas, now she was watching for possible moles.

How did a mole act?

Were they overtly sneaky and suspicious-like or did they smile at you in the cafeteria and offer to share their homemade banana bread like Yvette in Lab Three?

She was barely sleeping and her eyes were beginning to cross.

When her shift ended, she gratefully shut down her station, cleaned her lab and went straight home. She didn't even run through a drive-through to pick up food, because she just wanted to fall into her bed and forget how her life had been turned upside down.

She also wanted to forget that stupid ache in her heart whenever she thought of J.T.

Several times Hope had thought of calling Blue Yonder in the hopes that J.T. would pick up, but she chickened out before she could put the thought into motion.

What was she going to say to him?

"Sorry, I was a jerk and I really do care for you"? "Please come back and sleep beside me because I'm scared of my own damn shadow these days"?

It would be easy to cop out and say that the only reason she missed J.T. was that he made her feel safe during these weird times, but that wasn't it. He made her laugh, he drove her crazy and the sex was sublime.

The fact that he also made her feel safe was just a bonus.

Hope opened her front door and walked zombie-like to her bedroom, needing sleep and lots of it, but as she headed straight for her bed, something pushed her hard and she landed on the bed with a startled shriek.

She kicked out blindly and connected with a hard body as she tried scrambling away, but a hand grabbed her foot and pulled her back, cruel fingers biting into her ankle as she tried to kick herself free.

"Help!" she tried to scream, but her lungs were seizing with fear and nothing more than a terrified squeak came out. She kicked again and she was wrenched onto her feet by her hair as something hard pressed into her side.

"Kick me again, bitch, and I will put a bullet in your

gut. You won't die right away, but it will hurt so bad you will wish you were dead."

Shaking all over, she bit her lip to keep from crying out. Every self-defense rule she'd ever learned told her to scream, to take the chance because she had a better chance at survival if she attracted attention, but fear had paralyzed her vocal cords.

"Please don't kill me," she whispered. "Take whatever you want—just don't hurt me."

"You have a spare ten million lying around?" he sneered, and she froze. "Because that is what you owe me. Your little stunt cost me plenty and it is time you pay your dues."

"Who are you?"

"I'm crushed you don't recognize my voice, darling. I had such grand plans for you and me. I even considered making you my wife. Now I have different plans... Plans that are not so pleasant."

Anso DeLeon! How was it possible? "You're supposed to be d-dead."

"Sorry to disappoint. I'm difficult to kill, it seems. Now, here's how this is going to work. You're going to come with me like a good girl and finish the job or else I'm going to kill you right now."

"I destroyed the samples," she said, shaking. "There's nothing left."

He shoved the gun against her temple. "Well, then, you'd better hope you have a very good memory. Now *move!*"

It was dark. No one would notice Anso holding her tightly as they walked to his awaiting vehicle. It would look as if they were lovers going for a stroll.

Tears sprang to her eyes. This was what her pride had brought her—being kidnapped for a second time by a madman with nine lives, apparently. Why hadn't she listened to J.T. about Tessara? Why had she pushed him away?

"You were shot," she said, grimacing as he dug the gun into her side as they walked.

"Yes, I was. But I have excellent doctors on staff. I should tell you, I'm quite put out about the deaths of my guards. Your friend will pay for that. The charter business is filled with dangerous things lying around. Accidents happen."

Her heart stopped. "Leave him out of this. He's nothing to you."

"No one screws with Anso DeLeon, my girl. A lesson has to be taught."

"What are you going to do?"

"And spoil the surprise?" His chuckle made her want to pee herself. "I hope you're a fan of fireworks, because something is about to go boom."

J.T.! Tears sprang to her eyes as Anso stuffed her into the sleek Town Car and they drove off into the night.

J.T. PULLED UP to the apartment complex to see a black Town Car speeding off. The hairs on the back of his neck stood on end and he had a bad feeling. What was a Town Car doing in this neighborhood at this time of the night?

And why had it sped off like that?

Something wasn't right.

He bounded up the stairs to Hope's apartment and found the door open. His dread tripled when he checked her entire place and found it empty, but saw a sign of a struggle in the bedroom.

Shit!

J.T. bounded out the door and called Teagan as he ran back to his truck.

"Someone's taken Hope! I think she's in a black Town Car. Get Ty on the phone to check the surveillance cameras on Sutton Avenue at the intersection of Olive and Nabor Avenues! I need to know where that Town Car is going!"

"Shit, man, are you sure?"

"I feel it in my gut. There was a sign of a struggle and she's nowhere to be found."

Teagan didn't question and simply hung up to do as J.T. asked.

Ty called and J.T. immediately answered. "Where'd it go?"

"Turned down Magnolia at a high rate of speed, heading to the airport."

"Got it. We need back up on this. Does Harris still have connections to that FBI guy?"

"Yeah, I think so."

"Call him. Tell him everything we know so far. I'll do what I can, but if she gets on a plane, she'll be as good as gone."

"You got it, brother."

J.T. clicked off and pressed the gas pedal down harder. He had to make it to the airport. He cursed himself for hanging back, for sulking like a baby when he'd suspected there was still a threat at large.

What had he been thinking?

If anything happened to Hope… He couldn't think straight.

Flashbacks of his last tour threatened to send him off the road. He felt helpless, impotent rage, and his lungs squeezed every bit of air from his chest…

No! He would find her. He would save her.

Use your brain. Think. The fact that it was a Town Car said that whoever had snatched her had money, which meant they wouldn't fly commercial.

LAX had private planes coming and going all the time. Who had enough money to have their own private plane?

Anso DeLeon.

But he was dead.

He thought of that night and realized he hadn't actually seen Anso's body, just the word that Ricardo had shot him and then the guards had riddled Ricardo with bullets.

Anso was the only one with the means to pull something like this off. Plus, he was the only one with high enough stakes to risk being caught.

He called Teagan. "Find out which hangar is registered to Anso DeLeon," he instructed, taking a hard right for a shortcut to the airport.

"Hold on—let me check," Teagan said. Then he came back with "Hangar Twelve."

J.T. asked, "Did Harris call his FBI friend?"

"Yeah, rousted him out of bed. He thinks Harris is full of shit, but he managed to talk him into checking it out. I hope to God you're right. Otherwise, Harris just burned a pretty good bridge."

Yeah, he hoped so, too. "Ditto, brother."

He reached the airport and flashed his pilot license to gain access to the private charter area.

Picking up speed, he saw the Town Car parked in front of a waiting Learjet. He knew they couldn't take off until they had clearance, and by the looks of it they couldn't leave for another ten minutes.

He parked out of sight and ran the rest of the way, needing the element of surprise on his side.

J.T. was shocked to see a woman was holding Hope hostage. She was talking to her, but he couldn't exactly hear what they were saying.

Then he spotted Anso, exiting the car, directing the people stowing his luggage in the sleek plane.

J.T. ground his teeth, wishing he'd doubled back to make sure the man was dead.

But who was the woman?

The woman started arguing with Anso as Anso grabbed Hope by the arm and pulled her to him with sharp words directed at the woman.

He crept a little closer, praying his backup arrived soon.

He didn't dare risk going in guns blazing, but it took everything in him to stay put.

J.T. wasn't looking to be a hero, but he wasn't going to let Hope board that plane.

25

"I KNEW IT was you," Hope said to Deirdre, ignoring the bite of Anso's fingers into her arm. "I always knew you were a coldhearted bitch, but I didn't realize you were corrupt, too."

Deirdre ignored Hope, her eyes flashing with jealousy. "I told you we don't need her. I have her notes. I can replicate the results without her."

"Darling, I don't traffic in maybes. If you'd been able to replicate the results, we wouldn't be here now, would we? She's coming and that's final. If you have a problem with it, please, by all means, go home."

Deirdre paled, sputtering. "You know I can't do that. I risked everything to get you those notes. You promised me you would take me with you."

"Yes, well, if you stop bitching and moaning with your petty womanly complaints, then you may still come. I always like to have a backup," he said cruelly, and if Deirdre hadn't been such a terrible person, she might've felt sorry for her, but as it was, all she felt was rage.

"It was you. You got Tanya killed."

"Tanya got herself killed," Deirdre said, casting her a withering look. Good gracious, how had she never noticed how much Deirdre hated her? "She had an opportunity and she squandered it on useless morality. I was the one who approached her, so she had to go. No loose ends."

"You're an awful person." She looked to Anso. "Actually, you two are perfect for each other. Two peas in a rotten pod."

"Careful, darling—one does not need a tongue to do one's work," Anso warned, smiling when she shrank away from him. "But I'd hate to see that beautiful face of yours marred so terribly. Perhaps if you plead prettily, I will show you some mercy."

Hope tried not to cry. The threat of Anso "educating" her made her shake like a leaf with fear even though it shamed her that she couldn't spit in his face.

Her thoughts returned to J.T. and she sucked back a ragged sob. She wouldn't give Anso the satisfaction of seeing her cry. He'd all but said that he'd planted a bomb at Blue Yonder and she had no way of warning them.

Teagan, J.T., Kirk, Ty, Harris...they'd all risked their necks to save her and she was repaying them with a first-class ticket to heaven.

"You're a bastard," she whispered, and Anso laughed.

"Come. The pilot is ready for us." As they walked to the plane, he took a deep breath as if he were enjoying the night air. "I'd forgotten how invigorating it is to do your own work. I could've hired someone to get you, but I wanted the satisfaction of doing it myself, and I'm so glad I did. Reminds me of my younger days."

"Why am I not surprised that you come from a life of crime?" she quipped with a spurt of bravery. "I won't do what you're asking of me. I'll die first."

"You'd be surprised how motivating pain can be."

"You'd be surprised how fortifying hatred can be," she shot back with a calm she didn't feel.

Deirdre was practically burning a hole into Hope's back,

and it was apparent Anso had made romantic promises to the crusty bitch that he had no intention of fulfilling. If Deirdre were smart, she'd realize that Anso would likely kill her once they left the United States.

In Brazil, Anso was king and Deirdre was nothing.

Anso shoved her in front of him to the steps. She took the first step and sirens split the air as a bullet whizzed past, striking Deirdre in the leg.

Deirdre went down with a scream and Anso tried pushing Hope up the stairs, but she knew this was her one chance to get free, even if it meant risking injury. She would do anything to avoid getting on that plane!

J.T. TRIED TO wait, but he couldn't a moment longer. The police wouldn't get there in time to stop them from boarding, and if that happened, they'd never catch them.

He took careful aim and shot the woman in the leg, dropping her like a doe in the field.

Anso reacted by shoving Hope, but she fought back and J.T. started running toward them, using the fact that Hope was keeping Anso busy to cover more ground.

The woman was screaming, but Anso didn't seem to care. He was too focused on Hope to notice his companion was down.

Hope reared back and punched Anso right in the face, causing him to stagger and fall back, tripping on the woman and landing hard on his ass.

"You bitch!" Anso roared, struggling to his feet. But Hope didn't hesitate and kicked him in the face, bloodying his nose.

"Hope!" J.T. yelled as he ran toward her. *Almost there!* Hope's face lit up with joy and relief as she started to run toward him, but Anso grabbed her ankle as she ran past him, sending her sprawling to the pavement with a scream.

She kicked at Anso. "Let me go, you dickhead!" And

managed to grab the gun that'd skittered out of Anso's hands when he fell. She pointed the gun at his head, holding it with shaking fingers as J.T. caught up to her. "Let's see if you can stay dead this time!"

"Easy, babe," J.T. said, slowly easing the gun from her hand. "The police are on their way. You don't want to do this."

"Yes, I do," she said vehemently. "He deserves it. He deserves to die for what he did to me and what he did to Tanya and Carina and God knows how many more people. You know the justice system will let him walk!"

"He won't. We'll make sure of it," he promised as she reluctantly released the gun from her stiff fingers. "There's my girl…"

Realizing she was safe, she turned and buried her face against his chest, sobbing. He held her, but kept the gun trained on Anso and his accomplice. Until suddenly, she stiffened and cried, "Blue Yonder! He's planted a bomb! You have to tell Teagan to get out of there!"

The police skidded onto the tarmac and pulled out their guns just as J.T. was calling Teagan.

"Hands on your head!" a police officer shouted over a loudspeaker. "On the ground, all of you!"

"He's a madman! He shot me in the leg!" Deirdre screeched. "Help!"

"I want this man arrested," Anso said, trying to claim some authority. "He showed up and started shooting at us!"

"He kidnapped me and he planted a bomb at Blue Yonder Charter!" Hope cried out, refusing to be silent. "Someone needs to go check on Blue Yonder before the bomb goes off!"

"She's clearly crazy," Anso protested from his prone position on the ground as an officer handcuffed him. "I want to speak to my lawyer."

"Is this the guy you were talking about?" a man in a dark suit asked as Harris appeared with a shit-eating grin.

To J.T. he said, "I told you I had a friend in the FBI. You owe me twenty bucks. Danny-boy, this is my friend J.T., and yes, that's the man I was telling you about." Harris's voice rang out over the din of the airport. "That man is as corrupt as they come. Too much money, if you ask me. My mother always said money was the root of all evil and I said, well, my soul was for sale, and then she'd beat my ass for saying such blasphemy. Good woman, she was. God rest her soul. But this son of a bitch is a liar and a killer."

More police officers converged on the scene and after they concluded that J.T. was not the one who needed to be arrested, they took Deirdre away in an ambulance and Anso was taken into custody.

J.T. called Teagan as soon as he was able. "There's a bomb at the hangar. Don't go there. The bomb squad has to clear it first."

"Well, that's one way to get out of the biz," Teagan said. "Imagine the insurance payout. Maybe I ought to let it go up in smoke." He paused. "Did you get the girl?"

J.T. tightened his hold on Hope. "Yeah, I got her."

"Good. Now, don't be an idiot this time and don't let her go."

"Good advice, big brother."

Harris grinned up at J.T. and said, "Well, you're going to have to give me a ride because my buddy just left with the prisoner."

"How'd you convince him to show up? It must've sounded pretty crazy."

Harris laughed. "I told him if I was wrong, he could have my boat."

Hope's eyes widened. "You wagered your boat?"

J.T. frowned. "I didn't know you have a boat."

Harris's eyes twinkled. "I don't, but Danny-boy didn't

know that, now, did he?" He tapped his head. "Always gotta be thinking, boy. Always gotta be thinking."

"You missed your calling as a con artist," J.T. quipped, but Harris didn't take offense. If anything, the little bugger took it as a compliment.

"How about we get a drink and celebrate not dying… yet again?"

He looked to Hope and she gazed up at him, saying, "If you don't mind…I'd like J.T. to take me home."

That was all he needed to hear.

Slapping a twenty in Harris's hand, he said, "I'll take a rain check on that drink and you can take a cab."

And then he and Hope climbed into his truck and put everyone and everything in their rearview mirror.

26

J.T. COULDN'T STOP kissing Hope. It was as if he was afraid that if he stopped, she might disappear and he'd never be the same ever again.

He kept seeing Hope in Anso's grip, a gun pointed at her side, and he had to touch her to make sure she was safe.

She was still shaking by the time they reached her apartment. He held her tightly and she clung to him as if the world had nearly ended, because it almost had.

"I was so scared," she admitted in a soft voice. "I thought I was going to die."

"Never." He kissed the top of her head. "He can never hurt you again."

Hope nodded, accepting his assurances and lifted her face, her eyes glittering with tears. "Kiss me, J.T."

J.T. obliged, sinking into her kiss like a dying man. Their kiss quickly became urgent and their hands were shaking with the need to remove the clothing between them.

He would never get enough of this. Ever.

"Anso will have to get through me to get to you," he promised, pulling her shirt free and gazing at her beautiful breasts in the moonlight coming in through the window.

He cupped the fullness and bent to suckle the nipples as she threaded her fingers through his hair, moaning as he teased the tight buds.

They didn't trust words. Neither was looking to talk. They both knew how they felt about each another.

It didn't make sense, and on the surface, it was destined to fail, but there was something so electric about the way they were with each another that it was impossible to ignore.

He hoisted her into his arms and carried her to the bedroom. They tumbled to the bed and J.T. buried himself between her thighs, drinking in her sweet taste and loving every texture and nuance that made Hope uniquely beautiful.

J.T. refused to stop until he heard her breathy cries and felt her stiffen beneath his tongue. He would've loved to spend hours between her thighs, delighting in the way she moaned and lifted her hips to drive him deeper against her clit, but she climaxed quickly and he was forced to stop.

"That's no fair," he said in a husky voice. "I hadn't gotten my fill yet."

She grinned up at him and linked her arms around his neck, and he positioned himself at her entrance. Hope lifted her hips and he slid inside. For a blessed moment all he could do was sink into that wonderful, slick heat and groan with sheer pleasure. She clenched all around him, gripping his shaft with her internal muscles, and his eyes almost crossed.

"Hope," he gasped, her name like a prayer on his lips. He couldn't hold back. Damn, she was so hot he couldn't keep himself in check. "I'm going to come," he warned her, and she giggled, pulling him closer, burying his cock so deep inside her that they were nearly one.

And then he exploded.

"You are incredible," he breathed, sagging against her,

pressing soft kisses along her collarbone before rolling off her.

Hope snuggled up to him and the press of her body against his was the most sublime thing in the world.

"I think you've done the impossible," he said when he could finally speak.

"And what is that?"

"Domesticated me."

She laughed softly. "And why do you say that?"

"Because for the first time ever, I can't imagine wanting or being with anyone else. You're perfection and I never thought I'd ever find a woman like you."

"I'm not perfect," Hope said, tightening her arms around his midsection. "Trust me."

"You're perfect to me."

And it was true. He wasn't just spewing pretty words for her benefit. This was new for him. He was content to lie there with Hope, make love, talk, whatever. He was up for it all.

And it didn't scare him.

Actually, the more he thought of a future with Hope, the more excited about the future he became.

"How do you feel about kids?" he asked suddenly, shocking her into momentary silence.

"Kids?"

"Yeah, you know, tiny humans that look like you or me?"

"I know what kids are. Um, I guess I want them. Eventually. But not right now."

"Perfect. Glad to know we're on the same page."

Hope laughed and said, "One thing at a time. I might not even have a job to go back to."

He sobered and said, "When I got out of the Air Force, I was pretty messed up. I didn't want any attachments, because I didn't think it was fair to subject someone to my screwed-up past. And to be honest, I enjoyed playing the field. Until you."

Hope's gaze softened, but she remained silent, letting him speak his piece.

"I knew there was something about you from the moment I saw you. I didn't know it then, but I'd found the woman I was going to spend the rest of my life with."

She gasped. "Are you saying…?"

He kissed her fingertips and stopped at her ring finger. "If you would have me."

Hope climbed on top of him and smiled, a tear snaking down her cheek. "You better not be pulling my leg, because that's not funny if you are."

"I don't joke about that stuff. Too scary. I'm one hundred percent certain there's not a better woman out there for me. The only thing I worry about is if I'm good enough for you."

At that she dipped down and sealed her mouth to his in a fierce kiss. "You are more than good enough," she said, laughing through tears. "And we can spend our lives proving it to one another."

Sounded like an excellent plan.

He rolled her to her back, grinning as his heart—and other places—swelled. "So, about those kids…exactly what does *eventually* mean? Because I have this overwhelming urge to get you pregnant right *now.*"

Hope squealed with laughter and J.T. set about showing her just how determined he could be when he set his mind to something.

Particularly something enjoyable such as making love to his woman.

Yeah, *his* woman.

And that was that.

Epilogue

THE FOLLOWING DAYS were a blur.

"So tell me again how Deirdre knew Anso?" J.T. asked, linking his hands through hers as they laid in bed, twined in each other's arms.

"Apparently, Deirdre met Anso at a benefit, and when Anso learned of her high position within the company and the fact that she oversaw the virology department, he honeyed up to her. He convinced her that he loved her and that they were going to ride off into the sunset together in order to get her to compromise the lab."

"She must've freaked out when she heard he was supposedly dead."

"Anso must've contacted her soon after because she was pretty calm. She questioned me to see what I knew, and thankfully I heard your voice in my head cautioning me to remain quiet. It was the best thing I could've done."

J.T. grinned. "Glad to hear my voice in your head was a welcome thing."

"I missed you terribly," she admitted, closing her eyes as he brushed a kiss across her lips. "I never should've pushed you away."

"I never should've walked."

She smiled, her heart swelling with love. And yes, it was love. She knew that now.

"What's going to happen now?" Hope asked. "What if Anso's lawyers get him off?"

"That's not likely to happen. Now that Anso is in custody, they've been digging into his background and they've found all sorts of illegal activity they can prosecute."

"Good," Hope said. "I hope he gets sentenced to life in prison and he gets a bunk mate who makes him his bitch."

"So vicious," J.T. said, amused. "But I like it. You know, I was pretty impressed with that punch you landed on the tarmac and then that kick—wow. That was hot."

She snuggled up to him. "Well, I wish I'd found that spurt of courage when he attacked me in the bedroom. Maybe if I'd put up more of a fight, he wouldn't have managed to get me to the airport."

He gently lifted her chin to stare into her eyes. "Listen to me… You did exactly what you were able to do. Don't beat yourself up. You are the bravest, smartest and definitely sexiest woman alive, and I'll never let you forget it."

Hope warmed under his hungry gaze and sighed, knowing she'd never tire of this feeling. J.T. made her feel special and beautiful, sexy and dangerous in all the most wonderful ways.

Somehow she'd lucked out in the love department. She'd managed to find a man who made her hot and sweaty—in good ways—and was pretty damn smart, too.

She smiled and hoped Tanya was watching. Er…maybe not *watching*, but definitely smiling, because Hope had found the man no computer program would ever have been able to find. If only Tanya were still around to see her now.

Oh! And there was one more thing.

"I forgot to tell you," Hope said, rising on her elbow. "Tessara gave me a bonus and a promotion for my part in routing out Deirdre. I told you Tessara has changed. The company is really trying to change their image. They've even started a new committee on laboratory protocols so this never happens again."

"I'd still feel better if you got another job. I mean, there has to be a lab out there that would salivate to get someone of your caliber on their team."

This time Hope knew he was only looking out for her and instead of bristling at his suggestion, she smiled at his concern.

"How about you? What are you going to do about Blue Yonder?"

"Teagan changed his mind and wants to keep it going. I told him it was okay if we let it go, but he seems to think that I was right and that the business is going to turn around. The money we got from Tessara is going to keep us afloat for a while to figure out a new strategy."

She snuggled up to him. "Good. Because I was thinking… How long would it take to get to Cabo?"

He did a double take. "You want to go back to Mexico?"

"I figured it might be nice to see as a tourist this time. You know, instead of running for our lives, we could lie around on the beach and sip little drinks with umbrellas in them. Mexico was quite pretty when I wasn't jumping off waterfalls and being shot at."

J.T. hugged her tightly and she thrilled at how safe she felt in the cove of his embrace. "We'll go wherever you want," he promised, and she fell a little harder for the man she'd never seen coming, but wouldn't trade for the world.

Because, let's be honest, when a man like J. T. Carmichael came along, a smart woman held on.

And Hope was a very smart woman—she even had the PhD to prove it.

* * * * *

*Look for Teagan Carmichael's story
later in 2016! Available wherever
Harlequin Blaze books and ebooks are sold.*

COMING NEXT MONTH FROM

HARLEQUIN
Blaze

Available May 24, 2016

#895 COWBOY ALL NIGHT
Thunder Mountain Brotherhood
by Vicki Lewis Thompson

When Aria Danes hires a legendary horse trainer to work with her new foal, she isn't expecting sexy, easygoing Brant Ellison. But when they're together, it's too hot for either to maintain their cool!

#896 A SEAL'S DESIRE
Uniformly Hot!
by Tawny Weber

Petty Officer Christian "Cowboy" Laramie is the hero Sammie Jo Wilson always looked up to. When she needs his help, she finds out she is the only woman Laramie thinks is off-limits...but for how long?

#897 TURNING UP THE HEAT
Friends With Benefits
by Tanya Michaels

Pastry chef Phoebe Mars and sophisticated charmer Heath Jensen are only pretending to date in order to make Phoebe's ex jealous. But there's nothing pretend about the sexy heat between them!

#898 IN THE BOSS'S BED
by J. Margot Critch

Separating business and pleasure proves to be impossible for Maya Connor and Jamie Sellers. When they can't keep their passion out of the boardroom, scandal threatens to destroy everything they've worked for.

YOU CAN FIND MORE INFORMATION ON UPCOMING HARLEQUIN® TITLES, FREE EXCERPTS AND MORE AT WWW.HARLEQUIN.COM.

HBCNM0516

REQUEST YOUR FREE BOOKS!
2 FREE NOVELS PLUS 2 FREE GIFTS!

H HARLEQUIN®

Blaze

red-hot reads!

YES! Please send me 2 FREE Harlequin® Blaze® novels and my 2 FREE gifts (gifts are worth about $10). After receiving them, if I don't wish to receive any more books, I can return the shipping statement marked "cancel." If I don't cancel, I will receive 4 brand-new novels every month and be billed just $4.74 per book in the U.S. or $5.21 per book in Canada. That's a savings of at least 14% off the cover price. It's quite a bargain. Shipping and handling is just 50¢ per book in the U.S. and 75¢ per book in Canada.* I understand that accepting the 2 free books and gifts places me under no obligation to buy anything. I can always return a shipment and cancel at any time. Even if I never buy another book, the two free books and gifts are mine to keep forever.

150/350 HDN GH2D

Name _____ (PLEASE PRINT) _____

Address _____ Apt. # _____

City _____ State/Prov. _____ Zip/Postal Code _____

Signature (if under 18, a parent or guardian must sign)

Mail to the **Reader Service:**
IN U.S.A.: P.O. Box 1867, Buffalo, NY 14240-1867
IN CANADA: P.O. Box 609, Fort Erie, Ontario L2A 5X3

Want to try two free books from another line?
Call 1-800-873-8635 or visit www.ReaderService.com.

* Terms and prices subject to change without notice. Prices do not include applicable taxes. Sales tax applicable in N.Y. Canadian residents will be charged applicable taxes. Offer not valid in Quebec. This offer is limited to one order per household. Not valid for current subscribers to Harlequin Blaze books. All orders subject to credit approval. Credit or debit balances in a customer's account(s) may be offset by any other outstanding balance owed by or to the customer. Please allow 4 to 6 weeks for delivery. Offer available while quantities last.

Your Privacy—The Reader Service is committed to protecting your privacy. Our Privacy Policy is available online at www.ReaderService.com or upon request from the Reader Service.

We make a portion of our mailing list available to reputable third parties that offer products we believe may interest you. If you prefer that we not exchange your name with third parties, or if you wish to clarify or modify your communication preferences, please visit us at www.ReaderService.com/consumerschoice or write to us at Reader Service Preference Service, P.O. Box 9062, Buffalo, NY 14240-9062. Include your complete name and address.

He longed to reach for her, but instead he leaned into the van and snagged her hat. "You'll need this."

"Thanks." She settled the hat on her head—instant sexy cowgirl. "Let's go."

Somehow he managed to stop looking at her long enough to put his feet in motion. No doubt about it, he was hooked on her, and they'd only met yesterday.

If she was aware of his infatuation, she didn't let on as they walked into the barn. "I'm excited that we'll be taking him out today. I thought he might have to stay inside a little longer."

"Only if the weather had been nasty. But it's gorgeous." Like *you*. He'd almost said that out loud. Talk about cheesy compliments. "Cade and I already turned the other horses out into the far pasture, but we kept these two in the barn. We figured you should be here for Linus's big moment."

"Thank goodness you waited for me. I would have been crushed if I'd missed this."

"I wouldn't have let that happen." Okay, he was grand-standing a little, but it was true. Nobody at the ranch would have allowed Aria to miss watching Linus experience his first time outside.

"How about Rosie and Herb? Will they come watch?"

"You couldn't keep them away. A foal's first day in the pasture is special. Lexi and Cade are up at the house having breakfast with them, so they'll all come down in a bit." And he'd text them so they'd know she was here.

But not yet. He didn't foresee a lot of opportunities to be alone with her unless he created them. He wanted to savor this moment for a little while longer.

"Brant, can I ask a favor?" She paused and turned to him.

"Sure." He stopped walking.

Taking off her hat, she stepped toward him. "Would you please kiss me?"

With a groan he swept her up into his arms so fast she squeaked in surprise and his hat fell off…again. His mouth found hers and he thrust his tongue deep. His hands slid around her and when he lifted her up, she gave a little hop and wrapped her legs around his hips. Dear God, it felt good to wedge himself between her thighs.

Don't miss COWBOY ALL NIGHT
by New York Times *bestselling author*
Vicki Lewis Thompson, available June 2016 wherever
Harlequin® Blaze® books and ebooks are sold.

www.Harlequin.com

Whatever You're Into... Passionate Reads

Looking for more passionate reads from Harlequin®?
Fear not! Harlequin® Presents, Harlequin® Desire and
Harlequin® Blaze offer you irresistible romance stories
featuring powerful heroes.

♦HARLEQUIN *Presents*®

Do you want alpha males, decadent glamour and jet-set
lifestyles? Step into the sensational, sophisticated world of
Harlequin® Presents, where sinfully tempting heroes ignite a
fierce and wickedly irresistible passion!

♦HARLEQUIN *Desire*

Harlequin® Desire novels are powerful, passionate and
provocative contemporary romances set against a backdrop of
wealth, privilege and sweeping family saga. Alpha heroes with
a soft side meet strong-willed but vulnerable heroines amid a
dramatic world of divided loyalties, high-stakes conflict and
intense emotion.

♦HARLEQUIN *Blaze*

Harlequin® Blaze stories sizzle with strong heroines and
irresistible heroes playing the game of modern love and lust.
They're fun, sexy and always steamy.

Be sure to check out our full selection of books
within each series every month!

HPASSION2016

Reading Has Its Rewards

Earn **FREE BOOKS!**

Register at **Harlequin My Rewards** and submit your
Harlequin purchases from wherever you shop to earn
points for free books and other exclusive rewards.

Plus submit your purchases from now till May 30th
for a chance to win a $500 Visa Card*.

Visit **HarlequinMyRewards.com** today

MYR16R1